P9-DEZ-319

When I Was Your Age

◆ ◆ ◆

When I Was Your Age

✦

VOLUME TWO

Original Stories About
Growing Up

Edited by Amy Ehrlich

CANDLEWICK PRESS
CAMBRIDGE, MASSACHUSETTS

Introduction copyright © 1999 by Amy Ehrlich
"In the Blink of an Eye" copyright © 1999 by Norma Fox Mazer
"Food from the Outside" copyright © 1999 by Rita Williams-Garcia
"Interview with a Shrimp" copyright © 1999 by Paul Fleischman
"The Long Closet" copyright © 1999 by Jane Yolen
"How I Lost My Station in Life" copyright © 1999 by E. L. Konigsburg
"Bus Problems" copyright © 1999 by Howard Norman
"Pegasus for a Summer" copyright © 1999 by Michael J. Rosen
"Learning to Swim" copyright © 1999 by Kyoko Mori
"Waiting for Midnight" copyright © 1999 by Karen Hesse
"The Snapping Turtle" copyright © 1999 by Joseph Bruchac

All rights reserved. No part of this book may be reproduced,
transmitted, or stored in an information retrieval system
in any form or by any means, graphic, electronic, or mechanical,
including photocopying, taping, and recording, without prior
written permission from the publisher.

First paperback edition 2002

Library of Congress Cataloging-in-Publication Data is available.
Library of Congress Catalog Card Number 95-4820
ISBN 0-7636-0407-0 (hardcover)
ISBN 0-7636-1734-2 (paperback)

2 4 6 8 10 9 7 5 3 1

Printed in the United States of America

This book was typeset in Perpetua.

Candlewick Press
2067 Massachusetts Avenue
Cambridge, Massachusetts 02140

visit us at www.candlewick.com

CONTENTS

✦ ✦ ✦

INTRODUCTION

✦ ✦ ✦

When I Was Your Age, Volume Two has given me the great pleasure of editing a second group of stories by children's authors about growing up. I've now worked on twenty of these — twenty stories about twenty childhoods, twenty different ways of seeing and being in the world.

It stands to reason that every single person is unique, but when you ask twenty authors the same question: "What was it like when you were a child?" and get answers that are so wildly different in content and tone, it makes you look at other people in amazement. How have we come to be together? How do we even manage to communicate?

But the ten stories in *When I Was Your Age, Volume Two* (and those in the first volume as well) chart a clear and certain path through the forest of human differences. It is simply this: we are *all* different, we are *all* human, and if we tell the truth, we *will* be understood.

The authors in this collection have been honest and generous. They have shown us how they've managed not only to survive their childhoods but to treasure and even to laugh at them. If you read the notes at the end of each story, I think you will see an almost seamless connection between the authors' stories and the rest of their lives. These people—these children who grew up to be authors—write because they need to. By exploring the past with words, they can give form and meaning to their own experiences.

And what are these experiences? I think I can tell you a bit about each story without giving too much away. Rather than attempting to analyze anything, I'd rather tell you what I most love about each author's writing. That way, I'll be able to enjoy it all over again, and perhaps you will too.

Norma Fox Mazer's "In the Blink of an Eye" pulls us right into her world. Here is Norma, vivid from the very first sentence, all her nerves jangling: "In the gutter, a lit cigarette butt catches my eye. I swoop for it, stick it in my mouth, and take a puff. It tastes like dirty straw; still, I suck deeply, as I've seen my father do." Outside in the street Norma is tough, a tomboy, but at home she can't seem to stop crying. "There goes the faucet," her family say. "She's so sensitive . . . too sensitive." How lucky though for the rest of us that she was! It must be because Norma feels things so deeply that her writing is so full of feeling.

Rita Williams-Garcia, as we meet her in "Food from the Outside," is another case entirely. Her response to life is not to cry about it but to take action. Laughter, nerve, jive, and guile are how Rita, her brother, and her sister get around their strict, opinionated mother's rule never to eat at anyone else's house. Rita explains it with a comic's deadpan timing: "You see, our mother, known throughout the neighborhood as 'Miss Essie,' was still refining her cooking skills." The children's elaborate efforts to outsmart Miss Essie make their lives seem more fun and eventful than the situation comedies they watch on TV.

Paul Fleischman had no such obstacles to contend with. As he himself admits, "I lived in comfortable circumstances in beautiful Santa Monica, California, ten blocks from the beach, amid a loving family, in a time of peace . . ." *But* "all that meant nothing." Why? Because "throughout his school years he suffered from CSD, Chronic Stature Deficiency. Paul Fleischman was a 'shrimp.'"

I'm quoting from Paul's introduction to his story, "Interview with a Shrimp," which is set up in a journalistic question-and-answer format. To me, the fact that Paul has chosen such an approach to writing about his childhood confirms one effect of his shortness. Having a special vantage point, being *different*, helped to make him an original thinker—and eventually a writer.

Paul's story is also unusual in providing an overview of an entire childhood. Most of the stories in the book focus on a single dramatic incident, perhaps because that's the way experience is imprinted in our minds. Things that were upsetting or unresolved at the time stay with us.

Jane Yolen's "The Long Closet" is just such a memory—it begins with a mystery and ends with a terrible discovery. One night when she is sleeping in her grandparents' house in Virginia, an insistent, sighing sound wakes her. In this story—a tale of suspense, really—we are with Jane every moment, afraid to find out what the sound is, yet pulled forward by it. Everything is described with nerve-racking slowness. "The room was filled with that lovely, scary early morning half-light you get in the South; shadows of the tall pines seemed to creep around and about the wainscoting on the walls. The sound came again, and I realized it was coming from the long closet."

How does a writer re-create the past and give it over to us fresh and new and shining in the present moment? I think detail of the senses—what is seen, heard, smelled, *felt*—is the only answer. Draw a picture in words and make it real. This is just what Howard Norman does in "Bus Problems," when he describes the bookmobile in Grand Rapids, Michigan, where he worked every weekday in the summer of 1959.

We know just by the quality of Howard's writing—

and also because he does tell us so—that for him the bookmobile was an enchanted world, "a secure and peaceful place." We can see the leather benches mended with masking tape, and feel the heat of the day outside. It's as if the story has opened on an empty but familiar stage, then suddenly onto it leap the most amazing characters, and the drama begins.

If a child is lucky, there is always shelter, a place that is yours alone. For Michael J. Rosen, that place was on the back of a horse. "I'd climb in the saddle, and instantly, other riders, other horses in the ring, whatever it was I didn't want to do after camp or beginning in September . . . it all ceased to exist, along with the rest of my life on the ground, shrinking, fading behind the trail of dust the horse and I made heading to the horizon."

What I most appreciate though about Michael's story "Pegasus for a Summer" is the vulnerability and longing it conveys. He bravely wears his heart on his sleeve, letting us see so clearly his need for approval, for love.

All children certainly need these things, and the degree to which they get them, or don't, depends on their families. But children can sometimes be wrong about how their families feel about them, as E. L. Konigsburg wryly demonstrates in "How I Lost My Station in Life." There were two daughters in the family, Elaine (E. L.) and her sister Harriett, and it seems that Elaine's role was (1) to be the baby of the family and (2) to get all As in school. Everything was going along fine until (1) they moved in with relatives who had a child younger than she was and (2) she had to go to a new school, where the teacher ". . . asked the wrong questions for the answers I gave."

Behind the specifics of Elaine's plight is a bright child's need to do well—so that others will love her and also *for its own sake*. It is this latter aspect that can serve us, once we learn it, for our entire lives.

So many of the stories in the collection appear to be about achievement but aren't really. In Kyoko Mori's nearly bottomless "Learning to Swim" we easily understand her desire to please her wonderful mother by earning red or black lines on her bathing cap—each representing a certain number of meters swum in the school pool. The events in the story take place in Japan and there is a controlled, matter-of-fact tone to the writing that seems a part of this distant culture, yet we can still see in each speech and gesture all that her mother does for Kyoko and how deeply she is loved.

But what if a child's parents for some reason don't make the child *feel* loved? In that case, something truly amazing can still happen, as it does in Karen Hesse's "Waiting for Midnight." Unable to sleep at night, haunted by fears and her next-door neighbor's secrets, Karen turns to prayer. She witnesses what seems to be a miracle, and yet to me the *real* miracle is her own resourcefulness and the heartbreaking beauty of her imagination.

In "The Snapping Turtle" by Joseph Bruchac, beauty is outside and all around him. This is a story about nature, about a young boy's everyday intimacy with the world of plants and animals. Joe's grandparents, who raised him, gave him a good balance of things: his grandmother loved books and reading, and his grandfather schooled him in the ways of the forest and streams.

When he catches a snapping turtle one day while fishing for trout, his grandparents' response to his dilemma of what to do with the turtle makes it clear just how lucky he is in them: "My grandmother . . . looked at me. So did Grampa. It was wonderful how they could focus their attention on me in a way that made me feel they were ready to do whatever they could to help."

This response—to pay attention in a deep and careful way—is something that Joseph Bruchac and the other writers in this collection all seem to have learned as children. Their way of noting the details in a single moment and of feeling the pain and comedy and wonder of things are gifts to us.

As we read the stories, both moved and entertained, we may also be consoled. A girl who can't stop crying, three nervy kids in an African American family, a short boy growing up in California, a girl suddenly awakened in her grandparents' house, a midwestern boy with his first summer job, an elementary school scholar in the 1930s, a boy who loves horseback riding, a Japanese girl adrift, a lonely girl in Baltimore, a boy who is most at home outdoors—surely we recognize these children.

Surely they are like us after all.

—AMY EHRLICH

Norma Fox Mazer

• • •

In the Blink of an Eye

✦

NORMA FOX MAZER

I. Cigarette Butt

In the gutter, a lit cigarette butt catches my eye. I
swoop for it, stick it in my mouth, and take a puff. It
tastes like dirty straw; still, I suck deeply, as I've seen
my father do. I choke and cough, and my eyes stream
tears, as they so often do at home, but these are OK
tears, the kind you get from doing something forbidden and tough. My mother hates smoking. She says it's
a filthy habit; she calls cigarettes coffin nails, and
every time my father lights up, she says, "Oh, Mike!"
My sisters and I think she's prejudiced about cigarettes
and wish that she'd leave my father alone.

My sisters are Adele and Linda. We all have modern names, American names, interesting names. My
mother's name used to be Zlatckey. You can't even say

a name like that. Zlatckey! That was her name when she came to this country as a tiny girl with her parents and brothers. Then Zlatckey became Slats, but that was almost as bad, so she picked a new name, Jenny. That became Jeannie and then, in time, Jean. An OK name. It goes with my father's name, Michael, which is the best name in our family.

I let the butt drag from a corner of my mouth, the way my father does. Humphrey Bogart, the movie star, does the same thing. I think my dad looks a little like Humphrey, and they can both talk with the cigarette hanging from their lower lip. "How do you do?" I say, jutting my chin to keep the cigarette butt stuck on my lip. "My name is Norm——"

The butt slides off my lip and lands in the gutter again. Just as I bend down to retrieve it, I have a thought that makes my stomach jump. What if, behind one of the windows of one of the houses on this street, which is First Street in Glens Falls, New York, someone is watching me? And what if this someone, who is probably another mother, tells my mother she saw me smoking—and smoking not just a cigarette, but a cigarette *butt* that I picked up not just from the sidewalk, but from the gutter? The *filthy* gutter.

I walk away fast, humming and looking around brightly, as if I don't even know what the word *cigarette* means. But my breath is hot and stinky, a dead giveaway. I fan my mouth over and over. Then, from the other end of the street, I hear my sister calling me to supper. "Norma," she yells, "Normaaaa!" She's six years older than me and thinks she's my other mother. I'm not ready to answer and dawdle past Bud the Bicycle Man's repair shop. It's really just another little single-family house, with a sagging porch jammed with bicycles and bicycle parts. Inside, more bicycles hang from the walls and the ceiling. And there's Bud, with his grease-smeared overalls, who never says anything except "Ay-yuh" when you ask him to fix the chain on your bike or raise the seat.

Two doors down is the candy store, which is also a house with the store in front where the living room is supposed to be. I check all my pockets on the off chance that there's a penny that I missed spending. Two sisters with rolled gray hair own the store. They stand so perfectly straight behind the counter that I think maybe they sleep like that, ready in an instant to open their eyes and sell the next customer a Tootsie Roll or six gumdrops.

"Nor-maaa . . . Norma Fox!" In the authoritative slap of my sister's voice, I hear the bad news that she might already know that I've been — smoking. She has a way of intuiting things like that. And now it's not just my smelly cigarette breath that's hot, but my whole face.

II. The Street

"Your sister's calling you," someone says behind me.

It's Herbie Sternfeld, giving me one of his strange grins that seems to involve only half his face.

Herbie, his parents, and their shaggy St. Bernard live downstairs from us. They're our landlords, and my mother says I have to be polite to them. It's not hard to be polite to Herbie's parents. I like them. Being polite to Herbie is different, though. I don't know if I don't like him, or if I'm just scared of him. I don't know if I'm scared of him because he is scary or because he's weird.

It's not just his double-thick glasses or his awkward, neck-forward walk, or even his stiff black hair that looks like cartoon hair that somebody shot electricity through. It's the way he talks in a loud, uninflected voice, and how he spends his time, doing experiments with chemicals in the shed behind the Sternfelds' kitchen. And it's how sometimes he looks at you and says hello, but sometimes he looks at you and yells at you to get away, and sometimes, the worst, he flashes his eyes.

I hate it when he flashes his eyes. They're big and round and black, and they dart around and hardly ever seem to look straight at you, but then suddenly they'll light up and do that flashing thing, as if he's sending an important message. A vital message. A message you better get.

I'm surprised to see Herbie on the street. Sometimes he sits on the front porch and yells at people passing by, but he hardly ever goes out. Me, I'm always outside, playing every minute I can. Like all the other kids, I race through backyards at dusk playing hide-and-seek, listening for the call of "Alleee alleee infree!" I climb the crab apple tree on the side of our house to eat the sour, wrinkled little fruits, and I roller-skate and bike everywhere. I jump rope and play ball with the girls, and marbles with the boys, crooking my thumb and crowing when one of the dark no-nonsense shooties hits the mark.

"I'm going to the store," Herbie says. Shouts, really. "Getting bread for my mother. You like that white bread, huh, Fox girl?"

It's true I like the mushy, store-bought white bread the Sternfelds eat, the kind of bread my mother won't allow in our house because, she says, it isn't healthy. I know she must be right, but I also know how good mushy, store-bought white bread tastes, because I've eaten it, taken it right from Herbie's sweaty hand. I only did it once, but I also read one of Herbie's comics at the same time, which makes two bad things I did simultaneously. We don't read comics in our house, either.

"Norma!" my sister calls again briskly. "Norma Fox! Norm*aaa*! Supp-*er*!"

"Com-*ing*!" I call back, but I don't move. Herbie's staring at me: it's almost an eye flash, and maybe that's the reason I tell him I've been smoking. To distract him. To fend off that eye flash.

"Smoking?" he says in his loud voice. "You have not."

"I have!" I say, and with two fingers next to my mouth I demonstrate how I held the cigarette just like a movie hero.

Herbie peers at me through his thick glasses, as if I'm one of his experiments. "Dirty liar," he says.

My cheeks go hot. This is almost the worst insult anyone can give me. I lean into his face. "*Huuuuh!*" I breathe, and blow hot cigarette breath at him. "*Huuuuh!*"

He reels back as if I've shot him, one shoulder up defensively, then gives me a hard shove, sending me back against a tree. I hit my head, and it hurts! I want to cry, but I can't, because I'm outside. "You dumb sissy," I choke.

Herbie makes an ugly grimace and walks away. Maybe he didn't hear what I said. I cross fingers on both hands and run the rest of the way home, holding back the tears.

III. The Faucet

In the house, in my family, I cry a lot. I get my feelings hurt all the time. I cry if someone says something mean to me. I cry when I hear a sad story. When dirty Billy Miner knocks me down in the snow, falls on top of me, and shoves his lips on mine, I cry—but not outside. I wait until I get home. Then I cry agonies of humiliation. I cry when I lose my turquoise ring. I even cry—but only at home—if I don't get a good mark on a test.

Nobody likes my crying. "She cries at the drop of a hat," they say. "There she goes again. . . . Here come the waterworks. . . . Turn off the faucet, somebody!" Just seeing my eyes fill and my face get set to crumple is enough to bring on exasperated sighs. Sometimes I'm almost like two different people, the tomboy outside my house and the crybaby inside.

My baby sister never cries. She doesn't even care if you say, "I'm going to tell Daddy on you!" Nothing can make her cry. She just sticks out her tongue and laughs at you. A spatter of reddish freckles arches across the bridge of her nose, her little blonde braids stick out at an angle from her head, and she says things that are so funny the grownups repeat them to each other. She's fearless, kisses dogs, and tells everyone in first grade the Facts of Life, which I have only recently learned about, myself, from a book our mother gave me called *Let's Talk About Life*. (The first story in the book is about chickens and eggs. The next one is about frogs and eggs. Nothing becomes too clear to me from reading that book.)

My uncle calls my little sister Dynamite. We all have names besides our given ones. Older sister is the Bright One, the Beautiful One, the Good One. I'm the Too Sensitive One, the Tomboy, the Faucet. Younger sister is the Brat, the Mouthy One, and Dynamite, the best name of all.

My older sister is pretty much dynamite, herself. She has already done many good things in her life, such as always getting on the Honor Roll and, even when she was only six years old, making breakfast every morning for my mother. Of course she has a boyfriend. His name is Will, he has a big nose, and he's handsome, with white blonde hair sticking up like a Marine cut. I want him to notice me, and he does now and then, but mostly not. That's why sometimes I go in my room and cry, even when nothing has happened. My eyes swell, my cheeks get hot and tight, and then come the tears. "Crying again?" my mother says, looking in. Which makes me cry harder.

Every night, I promise myself I'm going to stop crying. I won't ever cry again. But I do. I can't help it. Every time something happens, I cry. And cry and cry.

I have been crying my way through the days, the weeks, the months. I cry rivers, lakes, and oceans of tears. "There goes the faucet," I hear. "She's so sensitive . . . too sensitive!" I start to hate my crying. It leaves me feeling weak and helpless, but what can I do? I don't ask for tears. They just come.

IV. Wonder Woman

My sister is waiting for me, standing near the Sternfelds' front porch, a kind of concrete apron with two pillars. Upstairs, right above it, we have a better porch too, where my mother lets us eat in summer. My sister puts her hands on her hips. "Where were you? What were you doing?"

"Nowhere. Nothing." I talk through tight lips.

"I was calling you."

"I know."

"Mom is home from work. She wants you for supper."

"I know."

"Were you with someone?"

"Who?"

"That's what I asked you."

"What?"

"Don't be fresh. Who do you think you are, Wonder Woman?"

"Yes, yes, I'm Wonder Woman!"

I forget to keep my lips tight, and she leans close and sniffs, her nostrils drawing up in disgust. "What's that nasty smell?"

I run around her, up the wooden steps into our apartment, and down the hall: past the room that I share with my little sister, past the door to the back stairs, then the living room and the kitchen, and into the bathroom. I lock the door and rinse my mouth repeatedly with cold water. The encounters with Herbie and my sister have upset me. I was tough, but I wanted to cry. And now I do. First I cry just a little, rubbing my shoulder and my head, where it hit the tree. I think how mad my mother's going to be if she finds out I smoked. I shouldn't have done it, especially not a filthy butt from the gutter, and maybe I'm going to die from all the germs. I cry harder. It's comforting in a horrible sort of way to feel the hot tears on my cheeks.

My mother knocks on the bathroom door. "Are you in there? Are you crying again?"

"No," I choke, and think how sorry they will all be when I die. Sad and sorry. They'll be the ones crying then. They'll appreciate me at last—so young, so dead.

At supper, I'm especially quiet and polite, so no one will notice my red eyes and ask if I've been crying again, and then notice me some more and wonder why my breath is stinky. But it's OK, anyway, because my parents are upset, too, and not paying attention to me. They're talking about Mr. and Mrs. Sternfeld, who might want to raise our rent. I don't think they will, because they're too nice. They're not at all like Herbie. They're both old and small with white, fluffy hair. They're quiet little people, and they smile when they see me and nod their little white heads and say, "Nice girl! Nice girl!"

That night, through my bedroom floor, I hear Herbie talking to his parents in his loud, excited voice. My little sister is sleeping in the opposite bed. Nothing wakes her up. Herbie's yelling now, and I feel scared for his parents. I wish I could go down there and zap him, like Wonder Woman. One zap for shoving me, one for yelling at his nice little parents.

V. Eyes

Every morning in the cold weather, before my father leaves for work, he runs down the back stairs from our apartment to the unheated shed on the ground floor. Sometimes I get up early and run down the stairs after him. In the shed, he pulls up the trap door in the floor, and we go down another flight of stairs into the cellar. It's dark down there. As my father feeds the banked night fire shovelfuls of coal, it leaps and roars into life inside the furnace. If Daddy's not in too big a hurry, he lets me dig into the coal bin and feed the glowing heart of fire. It's hard, heavy work, but I don't ever cry when we do this.

Nor do I cry when I play with my girlfriend Eva in the shed in warmer weather. Eva's the crybaby, then. She's chubby and always wants to play stupid things like Tea Party and never anything good like Spies. It's a new game I've made up. We have to be very quiet, which Eva doesn't like. We can't giggle or snort or make any sounds. She doesn't like that, either. And we can only play the game in our shed, because right next to it is the Sternfelds' shed, and we can't play the game without the Sternfelds' shed.

The way you play is this: tiptoe to the wall that separates the two sheds and press your eye against the wall where the thin vertical slats meet. If you get the right angle, you can see into the Sternfelds' shed, and if you're lucky, you can catch Herbie across the room, near the little window, mixing things in jars and beakers. And then—and this is the point of the game—you can make up stories about him. Sometimes he talks to himself. He makes noises and grunts. Sometimes he laughs. He's crazy, or might be a genius. Or both, I think. In comics and movies, mad-genius-scientists' eyes always flash like his. Plus, I notice, his lips are very, very red.

"So what!" Eva says, when I point this out. "It's boring."

She won't play any more with me. I don't really care, because I'm never bored when I make up my stories or watch Herbie through the slats. Sometimes it crosses my mind that this game is something else my mother wouldn't like me to do. *Stop*, I tell myself, but I don't. I don't want to stop.

Once or twice, Herbie looks toward the flimsy wall separating us, and seems to look at almost the exact spot where I've got my eye. It scares me. *Stop*, I say to myself again. But I go on making up stories about Herbie. I go on playing Spies. It's almost like crying, something I tell myself not to do, but do anyway, except that Spies is better. It's stories, like the books I read, but what's so good is that they're mine. No one can say anything about my stories, because no one knows about them. They're all in my head, like the chant I do every time before I play Spies—*Herbie be there*. And he is there, day after day, almost as if he knows what I'm doing and is a willing part of my game and my imagination.

One day, when I put my eye to the crack between the boards and peer into the Sternfelds' shed, Herbie is there again, but not across the room. He is right there, standing by the wall, staring back at me, his face puckered with concentration. He has a hypodermic needle in his hand. Faster than I can take in what's happening, he raises the needle and pushes the plunger. A stream of hot liquid shoots between the slats and into my eye.

For an instant, there's a stillness, as if nothing has happened. Words form in my mind. *She froze with terror.* I'm making up a story about this. That is the way to do it, to keep things from hurting. In the next instant, my eye begins to pulse and then to burn and hurt more than anything has ever hurt. I stumble up the back stairs, calling for my mother — my mother, I want my mother.

She sits me in a chair in the living room, the best chair, my father's reading chair. She wraps ice in a dishtowel for me to hold against my eye and runs to the phone. My eye feels as if it's held in place by the frailest of threads, as if any wrong movement will snap it free. I sit like a ramrod in the chair, focused on holding my eye in my head and the pain far back in my mind, where I can almost see it — a rush of blazing white. If I can keep the pain back there, in that white place, then my eye might also stay in place.

Soon the doctor comes. He produces a light from his bag and looks into my eye with it for a long time. Then Mrs. Sternfeld is there, squeezing her apron between her hands, patting my head and my shoulder. "She's good, a good girl," Mrs. Sternfeld says.

No, I think. I'm not interested in being a good girl. What I'm interested in is *not crying*. Since I ran up the stairs, I haven't uttered a word of complaint or shed a single tear. I don't understand exactly why I'm not crying. Maybe I don't want to cry in front of strangers. Or maybe this is too important for tears. Tears are the easy way, the way I've always gone, and now I've chosen — or been allowed — to take another way. Silence. Quietness. Waiting. Watching.

"Well," the doctor says at last, "a fraction closer, and she would have lost her sight in that eye."

His words make an immediate, deep impression on me, deeper than the pain, deeper than the fear or the memory of Herbie's resolved expression as he released the acid. In years to come, I never forget those words or lose a sense of gratitude that my sight was spared.

It may be from that moment that I begin to take the world in through my eyes with a special intensity. It is from that moment that I stop crying. Although I don't know it then, sitting in that chair in our living room, I have passed over a line — the invisible line between childhood and whatever it is that comes next. Not adulthood, not that quickly, but the beginning of the long, long walk into another world.

✦ ✦ ✦

◆ ◆ ◆

Notes from Norma Fox Mazer

"The years during which my family lived in a second
floor apartment on First Street in Glens Falls, New
York, stay in my memory as a series of sharp, brief
snapshots. To write 'In the Blink of an Eye,' I collected a
number of those snapshots and put them together to
see how they connected to one another and what their
greater meaning might be.

The events, both large and small, of the story, all
took place. I picked up a cigarette butt from the gutter,
played marbles with the boys, and ate raw rhubarb and
crab apples. I climbed trees, had a friend named Eva,
and went down into the cellar with my father in the
winter, where he let me shovel coal into the furnace.
My older sister called me to supper, and my younger
sister kissed dogs, and my mother sure did hate
smoking.

And, yes, our landlord's son shot acid into my eye
through that thin vertical space between the boards separating our shed from his. And the doctor was called,
and I didn't cry, and he said those words about my eyesight which I never forgot. The acid and the doctor happened in the same space of time, one morning or, more
likely, one afternoon (I've forgotten which), but did

everything in the story happen sequentially, one moment after another, the way things do in a story—in this story?

No. Our minds, our memories, are like erratic cameras. They snap quickly, this picture, not that one, another, then for days or weeks perhaps, not a single picture, then a whole series. It will be years after the moments we're all living through now before we discover which pictures were developed, which won't fade. And when we see these pictures in our mind's eye, we'll attach special significance to them.

I do, anyway. I think it means something that I remember the moment I stopped crying. And having written this story, I understand, for the first time, how that moment is linked to my having become a writer. Life is ultimately a mysterious unfolding of events. It's impossible for me, now, to imagine myself as anything but a writer. Still, I wonder . . . would I have become a writer if I'd gone on sobbing my way through life?"

✦　✦　✦

Bette William-Garcia

◆ ◆ ◆

Food from the Outside

✦

RITA WILLIAMS-GARCIA

My sister, brother, and I didn't have a dog, but we sure could have used one around dinnertime. Our dog would never have had to beg for table scraps, for we promised sincerely in our mealtime prayers always to feed Rover the main course. It wouldn't have been so much for love of dog, but for survival. You see, our mother, known throughout the neighborhood as "Miss Essie," was still refining her cooking skills. Until we could persuade our parents to let us have a dog, we sat at the dinner table with wax sandwich bags hidden in our pockets, especially when Miss Essie served "Hackensack," our code word for mystery stew.

"Rosalind, Russell, and Rita! Don't get up from that table 'til you eat every bit of that food," Miss Essie commanded. Then she'd stand there and not leave until we began eating.

Since we knew we'd be at the table for a long time, we came up with experiments to amuse ourselves while our parents watched television in the other room. Our favorite food test, the pork-chop drop, was devised by my eleven-year-old brother Russell, our resident scientist.

"Tonight we will continue our study on speed and density," Russell said, holding up his pork chop.

"I'll count, I'll count!" I volunteered, lowering my face to plate level.

Rosalind, the oldest at twelve, turned toward the living room to confirm that the coast was clear, then gave the "go ahead" for the pork-chop drop.

The object of the pork-chop drop was to compare the hardness of that night's pork chops to those of dinners past. Usually Russell would hold the chop about two feet above the plate and let it drop, while Rosalind or I counted the side-to-side reverberations of the pork chop as it hit the dinner plate. The thinner and harder the pork chop, the higher the drop count.

All we knew about food was what Mommy cooked, and the cold sandwiches and stewed spinach they served in the school cafeteria. Living in Seaside, California, we were separated by thousands of miles from our grandmothers, aunts, and cooking cousins who lived in New York, Virginia, and North Carolina. Eating in restaurants and fast-food places were frivolities we knew nothing of. Above all, we adhered to Miss Essie's firm rule, which was never to eat dinner at anyone else's house. She never gave a reason for her rule—other than the promise of a spanking, and we never thought to question her. As soon as our friends' fathers drove up to their driveways from work, we were to go straight home. Up until 1966, when we were twelve, eleven, and ten, Rosalind, Russell, and I believed that oil-soaked pork chops flattened to blackened sand dollars and cemented rice that defied separation was how food looked and tasted.

It was when Daddy replaced our black-and-white model with a color TV that we got an inkling about the texture and appearance of food from the outside, taste being the only missing component. We would sit in the dark before the glowing screen, oohing and aahing over a parade of McDonald's and Crisco Oil commercials, not to mention those sitcom dining-room scenes where platters of succulent meats and brightly hued vegetables graced the table.

"Mommy, how come our French fries don't look like that?" I'd exclaim, for ours were oily olive, dark brown, or black—certainly not golden brown and crinkled like the fries in the commercials.

"That's how white people cook," Mommy would reply, seemingly unaffected. Or, "That's not real—that's TV."

These answers worked initially, but being inquisitive

children, we began to ask our friends what they ate and how it tasted. We dared not ask them to smuggle out samples of their mothers' cooking—at least I didn't, believing Miss Essie was omniscient.

One thing was for certain. Daddy and Mommy didn't eat what we ate. They ate first and separately at some secret parent banquet where they drank Pepsi and laughed, and children were not allowed within earshot. To compound the mystery, Miss Essie did not permit us inside the kitchen while she was cooking their supper. We were to stay outside until she called us in for our own.

This only caused more speculation about what our parents ate and why we could not have any. Naturally we came up with a plan to investigate. The plan called for us to end our kickball game promptly at four-thirty in the afternoon. That was when Billie Holiday and Miss Essie sang "Ain't No Body's Business" while hot popping grease applauded in the kitchen.

"It's the only way," Rosalind insisted. "Me or Russell will do it. Pick one."

"Why *my* arm?" I wailed, limply offering it to her. "Why can't we use *your* arm?"

"Because you're the baby, and Mommy will do anything for her Rita Cakes."

I stuck out my tongue, rankled by a nickname that I had outgrown.

Rosalind yanked my forearm, then sucked hard until a red flower appeared on my skin. We stood back to admire it. Although it didn't swell as we had hoped, the red blotch was convincing.

Phase two of the plan then went into effect: As Agent X brought sobbing Agent Y in through the front door, Agent Z stationed himself at the back door, gateway to the kitchen. Just as Rosalind had predicted, Miss Essie dropped her potholder to attend to me.

"See, Mommy! A bee stung me."

Mommy, somewhat skeptical, inspected the fading wound, then took me into the bathroom for some first aid. This was all we needed to get our investigation of the grownups' food—or what Russell called the "fact-finding expedition"—under way.

We conferred at the dinner table that evening. Rosalind and I listened intently as Russell described the meats, vegetables, and starches he'd discovered.

"Sounds like chicken-fried steaks to me," Rosalind said.

"Chicken-fried steaks?" I gasped, unable to comprehend a two-meat dish or why anyone would want to eat it. All that chewing! I couldn't recall ever eating a steak, but was sure I wouldn't have liked it. And fried chicken always needed Kool-Aid to wash it down. I shuddered and asked my brother, "What else?"

"There were some beans in the small white pot."

"Yuck!"

"What color?" my sister wanted to know.

Russell put on his thoughtful face, imitating his hero, the colored engineer on *Mission: Impossible*. "I'd say, light brown with black round—"

"Black-eyed peas!" Rosalind cried, as if they were as good as pizza. "What else?"

"Vegetation of the dark green variety."

I loved the way my brother talked. He checked out almost every science book in our elementary school library and always entertained us with new facts and words.

"Boiled?" Rosalind asked.

"Beyond recognition," Russell replied. "With a piece of ham inside."

"Collard greens."

I grew nauseous. "Chicken-fried steak, black-eyed peas, and collard greens. Poor Daddy!"

"Yeah," Russell said.

Rosalind picked at her canned ravioli, then blurted, "I'd rather have that than this."

How could she say that? Ravioli was kid food with its own TV commercial. When was the last time you saw people on TV singing about chicken-fried steak and black-eyed peas?

. . .

The following evening we were not our usual selves at the dinner table. There was no talking, no food experiments, no laughter. Instead, we bit the bullet, quickly eating almost everything on our plates.

Once excused from the table, we reconvened in Russell's room. There, behind closed doors and out of earshot of our mother, we each produced a yellow school memo from our skirt pockets or shirt sleeves. These memos invited parents to bring their home cooking to our school's first ever International Food Fair.

Although we were veterans of Mommy's cooking, we did not want anyone else to sample those hardened pork chops and rice bricks. We would never live down our teachers' pity or our classmates' jokes. We agreed that Mommy could not know about the International Food Fair, let alone contribute a dish.

"Mommy won't find out about the fair unless *someone* squeals." Rosalind looked straight at me.

"If anyone squeals, I'll bet it's you," I said, convinced that my sister, the black-eyed pea lover, was becoming more adultlike every day. It was only a matter of time before she joined our parents' ranks and ate meals with them, leaving Russell and me at the kids' table.

Rosalind rolled her eyes, which Miss Essie expressly forbade. Eyeball-rolling was right up there with saying bad words and talking back.

"Ooh, I'm telling," I sang.

"I rest my case," she said. "Snitch."

"Red alert," Russell warned, hearing the thump of Miss Essie's bare feet as they headed toward the bedroom. Quickly Russell slid his school memo under his bed.

Rosalind and I sat on ours, arranging our skirts over our crossed legs.

Mommy opened the door without knocking. "There's cake on the table."

Normally those words created a rush for the door, but neither Rosalind nor I could get up. Russell, seizing his opportunity to choose the biggest slice of Mommy's pineapple pound cake, jumped up and bounded past Mommy for the kitchen. As soon as Mommy retired to her room, Rosalind and I raced after him for dessert.

"Why couldn't it be a bake sale?" Rosalind whined, for Miss Essie's cakes baked higher than Betty Crocker's and her rolls were softer than cafeteria rolls. "Why a food fair? An *International* Food Fair."

"We're not international," I said, trying to be helpful.

"We're colored," Russell told me, because that's what we called ourselves before 1968. That or Negro. "Everyone at school will expect Mommy to bring colored people's food."

"Maybe LaVerne's mother will do it. LaVerne is

always talking about her mother's barbecued chicken and ribs . . . how spicy and lip-smackin' good they are," Rosalind said, beaming.

Russell and I glanced at each other, then at her.

"You had LaVerne's mother's cooking!" Russell deduced.

"I'm telling!"

"You better not, or I'll get you, you little snitch!"

I mouthed "Oh, Mommeeee" at my sister, who flicked yellow icing at me, hitting me in the chest. I dabbed the icing with my finger and ate it.

Russell said, "Rachel's mother is making corned beef and cabbage."

"Rachel, Rachel, Russell likes Rachel," I sang.

Rachel O'Grady was a white girl in Russell's class with red hair and freckles all over her face. Russell was too dark to blush but his nostrils flared, making us laugh. That caused Miss Essie to holler, "All right in there!"

It was inevitable that one of us would flagrantly break the dinnertime rule and have to face Miss Essie. As it turned out, this was me. For our school's science exhibition I was paired with Yolanda Watson, the other colored girl in my class. We were at her house and had just finished constructing a weathervane to rival all weathervanes when her mother announced that it was dinnertime. Without thinking, I leaped up from the desk and grabbed my supplies.

"What are you doing?" Yolanda asked.

"I gotta be going," I said, as if Miss Essie was standing right there.

"Oh, but you must stay for dinner," her mother insisted.

"Oh no, I can't! Mommy said we can't eat no one else's cooking."

Mrs. Watson laughed and said, "Nonsense, child. I've made more than enough. Go wash up. I'll call your mother."

I could not wash my hands until I heard Mrs. Watson talking on the phone with my mother. Mrs. Watson was so hospitable, so insistent, that Mommy did the unexpected. She relented. I then washed my hands, certain of one thing: I was going to get a whipping that night. As clear as Miss Essie had always made herself about the dinnertime rule, I knew I wouldn't be able to sit for a week once I walked through our front door. But I was on the verge of tasting food from the outside, and that made me fearless. If I was going to get a whipping, it would be worth every snap of Mommy's belt.

We washed our hands and sat at the table. "What's for dinner?" I whispered to Yolanda.

When I heard the words, "fried chicken," my face

dropped. Yolanda and her mother exchanged "what's wrong with this colored child" glances, then asked what the matter was.

I knew better than to embarrass my mother with rude behavior and said, "Nothing, Miss Watson."

Yolanda's mother brought out a bowl of cooked cabbage, another bowl of mashed potatoes—the smell of butter wafting in the air—and a platter of golden-brown meat piled up in a pyramid.

"What's that?" I asked, pointing to the meat platter.

Yet another look was exchanged between the two. Yolanda poked me and said, "Fried chicken."

"Unh, unh," I disagreed, anxious to take my first bite. No sooner had "amen" sealed the blessing than my hand was all in the platter, reaching for a drumstick. I bit into it. The skin, a crunchy cornucopia of spices, set my palate a-dancing! I could not recall ever being so giddy at the dinner table. I tore into the golden-brown meat, savoring the juices, still remarkably in the tender white flesh.

Next I tried the peppered cabbage, surprising myself by stabbing and eating leaf after leaf. I wondered if the other cooked, soggy vegetables that I'd hated all my life could taste as delicious as the cabbage. My mind reeled.

"Gravy?" Yolanda offered, as I ate my first bite of the mashed potatoes.

"No way!" I exclaimed, knowing she could not possibly understand the sacrilege of pouring gravy over food as heavenly as this. Besides, I wanted to remember each distinct flavor of Mrs. Watson's mashed potatoes, which were creamy but not mushy, bathed in butter and dotted with bits of onion. I ate four more pieces of chicken, then marched happily home. After Yolanda and her mother moved away and those Kentucky Fried Chicken commercials began to air on TV, I was convinced Mrs. Watson was the *real* Colonel Sanders and my friend Yolanda was the KFC heiress.

That night, having gladly taken a beating for breaking the dinner rule, I earned my sister and brother's respect. I also earned their envy as I described every crunchy, spicy, tender bite of what I now knew was fried chicken. My only regret was that I could not have shared the meal itself with my sister and brother.

Finally my sister's envy turned to outrage. "If the squirt can get food from the outside, then all of us can get food from the outside," she said.

"And just how do we do that?" Russell asked.

"By going to the International Food Fair. It's our only chance to eat other people's food. *Good* food. Just imagine . . . barbecued spare ribs—the way they're supposed to taste."

"Corned beef and cabbage," Russell said.

"And fried chicken," I added. "But how can we get there?"

Rosalind said, "Mommy will take us."

"Are you crazy?" Russell and I exclaimed, one after the other.

Even though the door was closed, Rosalind felt the need to whisper. "Russell, do you still have your school memo? The one about the food fair?"

He found it underneath his bed.

"Good," Rosalind said. "Now, what is the one thing Mommy can make?"

I shot my hand up. "I know! I know! Rolls and cakes! Rolls and cakes!"

It was not long before we were huddled into planning formation, humming the *Mission: Impossible* theme.

In her best handwriting, Agent X drafted a new school memo announcing a shortage of dishes needed for the International Food Fair—biscuits, rolls, cakes, and Kool-Aid. At Agent Z's suggestion, Agent X added French and German dishes—entrees Miss Essie would not attempt. As agent Y, my part was to leave the "school memo" on the table along with our homework for our mother's inspection.

On the morning of the International Food Fair Miss Essie told us to keep our school clothes on all day because we were going to the program at the school.

My sister, brother, and I were as jubilant as looting

thieves. We could barely contain ourselves, anticipating the tables of prepared dishes from all over the world. Our friends were equally eager to sample our mother's cakes and rolls, since we had spent a good part of the day bragging about Miss Essie's delicious baked goods.

We rushed home from school and finished our homework in record time. Instead of our usual kickball game, we played cards out on the patio to preserve our school clothes. In between hands of casino we talked of nothing but the food fair and which tables we would visit.

Then five o'clock came. Miss Essie called our names, and we came running. With no time to lose we washed our hands and lined up in the kitchen to help her with the cakes and rolls. Miss Essie was ready for us. In our hands she placed three warm aluminum pans, tightly wrapped with foil.

Somehow the shape of the tins did not seem right for cakes or rolls. I who had once earned the nickname Rita Cakes could not detect vanilla, coconut, frosting, or butter anywhere. I raised the aluminum pan to my nose, took a sniff, and said, "Mommy, this don't smell like butter rolls or cake."

"That's 'cause they're pork chops," Miss Essie said. "Now let's go."

✦ ✦ ✦

Notes from Rita Williams-Garcia

"'Food from the Outside' is one story of mine that Miss Essie will never read because its truth outweighs the fiction. Even now, my sister, brother, and I often relive those days of sitting at the dining-room table before plates of pork chops or heaping bowls of 'Hackensack,' conducting experiments.

When we weren't playing with our food, we dreamt about our futures. Rosalind wanted to be an artist, Russell, an aerospace engineer, and I wanted to write stories. My allowance went to purchasing notebooks, postage, envelopes, and erasable typing paper. By age twelve, I was sending out stories to magazines and book publishers. When the rejection letters came in, Rosalind and Russell amused themselves by reading them aloud at the table, substituting their own versions of the editors' polite words of rejection. (Older siblings can be cruel!)

A year later I sold my first story to *Highlights for Children*. My mother divided the money among the three of us, and we went shopping for school clothes. After that, Rosalind and Russell would ask me during dinner if I had sent out any more stories."

✦ ✦ ✦

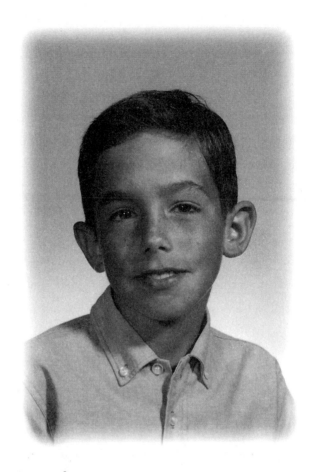

Paul Fleischman

◆ ◆ ◆

Interview with a Shrimp

◆

PAUL FLEISCHMAN

He arrives wearing a maroon corduroy shirt and corduroy pants. Has he chosen this fabric for its vertical lines, in hopes of looking taller? We shake hands. He appears to be about five feet six. Though sitting down would soften our inequalities of height, he seems in no hurry to take his seat. His speech and manner are confident. One would hardly guess the secret he'd revealed to me by phone and which I've chosen as the focus of our chat — that throughout his school years he suffered from CSD, Chronic Stature Deficiency. Paul Fleischman was a "shrimp."

How small were you as a child?

I was the smallest boy in the entire first grade. Likewise, in the second, third, fourth, fifth, and sixth grades. When I went to junior high school, I was the smallest boy out of a student body of a thousand. The name *Paul* means "small" in Latin. My parents chose well.

Clearly, a severe case of CSD. How important was your size to you at the time?

It seemed the first and foremost fact about me, instantly known to all observers. It was my definition, my central quality—and I hated it. I felt myself to be a modern Job, punished by an inscrutable God. That I lived in comfortable circumstances in beautiful Santa Monica, California, ten blocks from the beach, amid a loving family, in a time of peace—all that meant nothing. I would have traded another world war for six inches.

Millions of young men forced back into service, cities in flames, the world economy disrupted?

Actually, it's not so far-fetched. Napoleon was a super-shrimp who tried to conquer all of Europe, at a cost of millions of lives, to prove to the world that he was really Mr. Big.

And then there was Mussolini, the Italian dictator, in the 1930s.

Another world leader who never tried out for the N.B.A.

And then there was you — president of Roosevelt Elementary School, vice president of your junior-high homeroom, then president.

With plans to take over all of southern California.

Obviously, being small didn't hold you back. When did you feel the disadvantages of your height?

Staring at a tall adult's belt buckle. Standing at the blackboard in math class, working a problem next to a girl a foot and a half taller. Being placed in the front row and at the end of the line in every group photo. At my junior high school — grades seven through nine — the ninth-graders had been granted a raised patio called the Ninth Grade Walk. Any intruder from the lower grades could be expelled from it — or, more dramatically, thrown over the wall into the bushes below. I *never once* set foot there, even when I became a ninth-grader myself, for fear of being taken for a seventh-grader and hurled over the battlements.

The worst, however, was the humiliation that took

place in junior-high P.E. at the start of every semester. All the boys sat in their underwear in the gym, waiting to be called forward to be publicly measured, weighed, and assigned a letter—*A* for the big kids, *B* or *C* for the moderately endowed, *D* for the runts like myself. Naturally, these vital statistics were read into a microphone so that the muscle-bound coach across the room could scrawl them on a card. It was a scene reminiscent of slave auctions and the inspections at Auschwitz. I dreaded these events for a month beforehand. They happened twice a year—six times altogether in junior high. "Only four more left," I'd tell myself.

Did your smallness loom as large to other kids as it did to you?

Yes and no. I've brought along my junior-high yearbooks. Have a look at the inscriptions.

"Stay out of dark bars and taverns, and grow a little this summer."

"You're one of the few who make me look big."

"Remember to stay out of tall grass (one inch high) or you will get lost." Obviously, there was little public sensitivity to CSD at the time.

On the other hand, I had several friends who towered over me. Kids, it's often said, are cruel. But some kids can also be wonderfully oblivious of differences that rivet others. Mark Scott was a friend of mine whose stilt walker's stature probably derived from his habit of drinking an entire quart of milk in one gulp. People might have smirked seeing us side by side, but neither of us was bothered by the height difference. We were focused on the business at hand—skateboarding, calling Dial-a-Prayer on the telephone, scouring the laundromat floor for dropped coins.

What were your defenses against teasing?

In the classroom, brains and wit. I was "the little guy with the big brain." I won my sixth-grade class's scholarship award. Brains earn respect, but I was liked for being funny. I wrote a joke book with a friend in third grade. I pored over *MAD* magazines like a Biblical scholar, even punching holes in them and carrying them in my binder. In junior high, where three elementary schools converged, I met a group of fellow *MAD* fanatics—the sharp, wisecracking pack of friends I traveled among all the way through high school.

What about out on the playground?

Speed and coordination were my compensations for being small and weak. I avoided football and concentrated on tennis, which I was good at. Stealing and passing were my fortes in basketball. My friends and I developed a style of play in which we controlled the ball for long stretches of time, pretending to shoot but passing at the last instant. Then, we'd sink a basket and win two to nothing. It drove opponents crazy.

And then there were the made-up games.

Can you explain?

Those were games my friends and I invented that were actually parodies of standard sports. The longest lasting was "skrugby," which was football played with the banana-shaped fruit of a plant that grew in one of my friends' yard. We used the sort of fancy terminology that goes with traditional sports—arcane names for maneuvers, cryptic signals, complex scoring systems. The great thing about skrugby was that only we—not the school jocks—knew how to play it. We were very selective about admitting new players. When we'd stripped all the fruit from the plants at my friend's, we began using two socks rolled into a ball. At the same time, we used the word "skrugby" for another made-up game, namely soccer played with a chalk eraser in front of the tennis backboards. In high school, when several of us founded an underground newspaper— another alternate, satiric world—we reported on skrugby games just as the official school paper reported on football.

Did you follow professional sports or only make fun of them?

I was a big Dodgers fan, not just because I lived in Los Angeles but because of their style of play. They used speed and brains instead of brawn. Maury Wills, my hero, was their leadoff hitter — small, fast, and an expert base-stealer. An infield hit, a steal, another steal, a sacrifice, and out of nothing they'd made a run. The Yankees, by contrast, were Goliath, with Roger Maris and Mickey Mantle bashing home runs. I loathed them. In football, the Los Angeles Rams had a player like Maury Wills, a short, squirmy running back named Dick Bass who slipped through tacklers' hands like a fish. It was a joy to watch him slither out of their grasps. It was the revenge of the small, the triumph of Charlie Chaplin over the hulking policeman.

One of the tragic side effects of CSD is loss of confidence regarding the opposite sex. How did your size affect your interaction with girls?

Grammar-school boys pay little attention to girls, but I did, for the simple reason that there was always one girl in my class who was shorter than I was. For several years Sally Stewart filled this role. I wasn't religious, but prayed she'd never move away. In junior high, when girls shot up like June cornstalks, the contrast between most of them and me became comical. I still remember hurrying out of a classroom, rounding a corner at a run, and smacking straight into an Amazon of a ninth-grader. She barely budged; the collision knocked me to the ground. I got up and tried to disappear, recalling the advice of Laurel to Hardy in one of their movies: "Act nonchalant."

I had no girlfriends during junior high. I went to a total of two or three school dances. Though I got good grades, I would have failed the test of sexual experience that kids used to give each other, awarding five points if you'd kissed (eight for kissing underwater, ten for French kissing), fifteen points if you'd—you get the idea. Strangely, not all short boys fell into my category. There were pint-sized tough boys, more muscled than I, who executed vicious tackles in football, smoked—despite tobacco's reputation for stunting— and scored As on the sex tests. I listened to their accounts in awe. It was inspiring. Maybe the short could inherit a bit of the earth after all.

What happened when you reached high school?

Two things. Intelligence, creativity, life experience, political awareness—more and more, these outshadowed looks. And then, when it no longer mattered so much, I grew. Not a lot, but enough so that I no longer stood out so much. I realized that I wasn't Job. Instead of being cursed, I'd actually been blessed with all the things that really mattered.

What advice do you have for today's vertically challenged?

Stand tall! You'll survive and prosper in the end. And you'll be much more comfortable in cramped airplane seats.

✦ ✦ ✦

✦ ✦ ✦

Notes from Paul Fleischman

"Being short led naturally into being a writer for me. It was clear that I'd make my living with my brains, not my body. I wrote my first stories in grammar school—the adventures of two Chinese mice, the tale of an icc-age boy who thaws out in the present, a hilarious (so I thought) comedy titled *The Colonels on the Corn*. My father, Sid Fleischman, switched from writing adult books to children's books at this time. From his works—read aloud chapter by chapter, as they were written—I absorbed the pleasure of plot, the joy of playing with words, the stranger-than-fiction quirks of history.

Though my case of CSD lifted long ago, the experience casts a long shadow in my memory and has surfaced, in disguised form, in several of my books. Aaron in *The Half-A-Moon Inn* has a major physical problem to deal with, a different one than mine—he's mute. *Saturnalia* concerns a holiday in which the world is turned upside-down, with little children commanding their parents. It's a notion that appeals especially to the small and powerless. In *A Fate Totally Worse Than Death,* I took my gleeful revenge on the tall, wealthy, female aristocracy of my high school. Most recently, *Weslandia* stars a grammar-school misfit who develops his own alternate civilization in his backyard, exactly as my childhood friends and I invented our own games. Exactly as I still make up alternate worlds—short stories, novels, poems—today."

✦ ✦ ✦

The Long Closet

✦

JANE YOLEN

At my grandparents' home there was a long closet
that had two entrances. One was in the room my
brother Stevie and I shared at the back end of the house;
the other opened into my grandparents' bedroom in the
front. You could sneak all the way through the closet,
under my pinafores and Stevie's short pants without
touching a thing. But at the other end it meant dodg-
ing around Grandma's dozen flowered cotton housedresses that tended to wrap around your shoulders
and hold you fast, or her muzzy, full-length fur coat
that was like some large animal waiting to pounce.
And it meant stepping over Grandpa's ugly work
boots that were larger than any shoes I had ever seen,
with their leather strings turned black with wear.

We played in that closet during our long Virginia
sojourn, my brother and cousins and I. Some games
were familiar ones that I knew from New York City

like Hide-and-Seek, Sardines, and Tag. There was also a game we made up on the spot called Split, which had rules that changed whenever friends came to visit. Split was Hide-and-Seek in pairs, and the only thing unchangeable about it was that Michael and I, who were the oldest cousins, were not allowed to pair up together. We were too canny, too familiar with the hiding places, and too stubborn to be found.

The long closet smelled of cedar and mothballs, and something else, a heavier, homier smell that I realized years afterward had been my grandfather's sweat. My grandmother didn't have any particular smell, except perhaps a sweet talc scent; it was not a strong recognizable smell at any rate. Only later, when she was all alone and had taken up sucking on lemons, did she have a signature odor. To this day I smell a lemon and I think of her. But not then, not in the long closet. Not in the time I am going to tell you about.

We often visited Grandpa Dan and Grandma Fanny's little two story brick house under the whispering sycamores, staying for ten days in the summer. It was a wonderful place for a holiday, with the Hampton Roads, a part of Chesapeake Bay, just a short walk away. There were many children close to my age living up and down the block. On soft summer nights you could hear their mothers calling them home, the names like a southern anthem sung into the dusk.

Across the street was a family with four girls: Mary Beth, Mary Louise, Mary Alice, and Alice. Several houses down were Frances, Willard A, and Bubba. I developed a southern accent, just to fit in, losing it as soon as we got home again.

But the time this story begins was in the 1940s, during World War II. My father had joined the army as a Second Lieutenant and was being sent overseas. So we moved down from New York City to Hampton, Virginia, to the house where my mother had grown up. We would be spending the war years there, safe with Grandpa Dan and Grandma.

It had not been an easy decision. My mother—a small and darkly beautiful woman, who was shy with strangers but forthright with friends—had to pack up all our belongings in the sunny apartment overlooking Central Park, and cart us down to Virginia on her own. Daddy was off in boot camp and not able to help settle us in. As the third child of six, Mommy had long ago carved out her own life away from her close-knit and confining southern family. Returning home was for her a kind of defeat. But the war meant sacrifices of a much greater sort for other people. She never let us know how much she longed to be back in the great brawling city she had adopted for her own.

Daddy came to visit for a week and then shipped overseas. We went to see him off on a big boat from

Newport News, and then settled in happily with our grandparents. Only Mommy seemed to miss Daddy horribly from the start; Stevie and I were too pleased to be surrounded by our extended family, all of whom indulged us more than our absent father ever had. In fact, Daddy seemed more present now that he was away, because he sent letters home every week that Mommy read aloud to us. She pretended the letters were for all of us, but I could read the greeting. It always said "Dear Isabelle." It never mentioned Stevie or me.

Daddy wrote how he was winning the war single-handedly. I mistook this story-telling ability for the truth. It was ten years before I understood he hadn't even been in the fighting. He was a foreign correspondent, a newspaperman in khaki. When he came back to Virginia with a shoulder wound because he had been in London during the German buzz bomb attacks, it was convincing evidence of what a great warrior he had been. He played it for all it was worth, wearing his uniform for days after returning home, and keeping his arm in its sling long past any medical necessity. In fact, he never got to shoot a gun.

Grandpa Dan was a handsome, smiling man who always had time for his grandchildren—Michael and Linda one town over, and Stevie and me right there in his house. He owned a clothing store downtown, working long hours. But whenever he was at home, he enjoyed showing us how to use the tools in the garage, telling us stories, fixing the tree house in the yard. Grandma, with her white braids piled up on her head like a crown, was several years older than Grandpa Dan, but hated anyone knowing it. So we were never sure when she had actually been born. It made birthday celebrations odd to say the least. She was a bit more distant than Grandpa Dan, and she never told stories, but she walked the long block every evening. Anyone who wanted to walk with her or to work with her in the kitchen would get her full attention, but otherwise she was not exactly attentive.

After two tries at going around the block with her — she was the fastest walker I had ever known — I took the kitchen route. My favorite chore was chopping the apples for applesauce in Grandma's big wooden bowl. The chopper had a wooden handle and a dark, curved knife, like a scimitar I thought, like ones I'd read about in stories from *Arabian Nights*. *Chop, chop, chop.* I was Ali Baba and Sinbad and Sheherazade, sitting on the kitchen table and bending over the bowl. *Chop, chop, chop.* Friday night my cousins and Aunt Cecily and Uncle Eddie came for Sabbath dinner. *Chop, chop, chop.* We got to sit in the dining room at the big mahogany table with the grownups. *Chop, chop, chop.* And afterward we played outside in the limpid summer nights, the fireflies winking on and off. It stayed light in the summertime till past nine.

During the warm days, the neighbors' children and I played Chase-the-Dog, teasing a long-suffering mutt called Wowser. Wowser would take our pokes and whistles for a long time; he really had a lovely disposition. But finally he would have enough, rising heavily onto stubby legs to chase after us, whuffling like the Jabberwock out of Wonderland. At that we would all scatter, running and screaming with terror and delight. The older kids could climb a low projecting branch of one of the sycamores to get away from Wowser. But I was too short to get up without help. Mary Louise had to lean down and haul me up before Wowser got there. No one was ever bitten, though Wowser certainly had ample time and opportunity.

The one time I ever remember Mommy, Grandpa Dan, and Grandma acting together was the day Stevie got his first haircut. Mommy and Grandma protested because he had the sweetest head of golden curls imaginable. But he was already almost three years old and Grandpa Dan insisted. "This is no boy!" he said.

Grandpa sat Stevie on a silver-colored washtub that was upended on the lawn and, kneeling down next to it, proceeded to sheer off Stevie's curls. Mommy started crying, and Grandma wept as if her heart were broken, but the little golden curls floated down like angel wings to lie nestled in the green grass.

Stevie's lower lip began to tremble, not because the haircut hurt, but because Mommy and Grandma were making such a fuss.

"There!" Grandpa Dan remarked. "A proper boy." He picked Stevie up and carried him around on his shoulders for several minutes, calling out, "A proper boy! A proper boy!" Stevie loved that part and began giggling.

I gathered up the curls, as many as I could that had not been blown away by the breeze. My mother kept one in her wallet for years.

And then one morning everything changed.

I woke up early because I heard a funny sound in my bedroom. It had intruded itself into my dream: a kind of sighing, like the wind through the sycamores. And it repeated and repeated, with a peculiar insistence—an awful sound.

I thought at first Stevie was having a nightmare, but he was fast asleep in the bed across from mine, his snores coming in little *pop-pop-pops*.

The room was filled with that lovely, scary early morning half-light you get in the South; shadows of the tall pines seemed to creep around and about the wainscoting on the walls. The sound came again, and I realized it was coming from the long closet.

I began to tremble.

Now I was not normally a frightened child. My daring in games, in running last from the dog, in following the older children wherever they led, was already a legend all the way up to Kicoughtan Road. "Dare Janie," the local children would tell one another. "See what she's gonna do." But this sound made me shiver. There was something almost inhuman about it.

I knew it couldn't possibly be a ghost or a monster. I didn't actually believe in such things, though I loved reading about them. And besides, it was morning, not midnight. But it was a sound that had such desperation, such loneliness, such sorrow in it, as if the house itself were weeping, that I knew—without really understanding why—that shivering was the only reasonable response to it.

I don't know how long I lay in bed, hoping that Stevie would wake up so we could listen to the sound together. Then I could play big sister and calm his fears and mine at the same time. But he didn't wake. He just slept on and on, with that quiet little *pop-pop-pop* snore.

"I dare you . . . ," I whispered to myself. And then I got up. Slowly I walked over to the long closet, my bare feet dragging along the splintery wooden floor.

When I reached the closet—ten long steps from my bed—I put my ear against the door.

The sound was louder there—a moaning, a groaning so powerful it seemed to shake the wood.

Trembling so hard I thought I might actually faint, I eased the closet door open and went in.

Cedar and mothballs and that heavier, mustier smell enveloped me. Silently I walked under Stevie's clothes and mine, pulled along by a curiosity that was greater than fear. I came to the long winter coat that marked the beginning of my grandparents' things. Grandma's fox stole that I so loved to stroke brushed my face. This time it brought me not the slightest bit of pleasure. Grandpa's heavy serge suits, two of them that he wore only on the High Holy Days when he went to synagogue, stopped me for a moment. I pushed them aside and stepped carefully over his work boots.

The awful sound was coming in waves now. I pushed past my grandmother's soft, silky crepe Sabbath dress. Then I got tangled for a moment in one of her cotton housedresses.

It was pitch dark in the long closet because my grandparents' door was closed, but I knew where I was by the feel of every dress and suit. Dragged along by that heavy rope of sound, by the rise and fall of it, I pushed open the door.

And blinked in the sudden light. The sound was

coming from the window. I turned to see my grandmother sitting in the rocking chair, staring out at the dawn. Her white braids hung down her back. She was wearing a flowered housedress. The awful moaning cry was coming from her. I didn't know what it meant.

Grandpa was still lying on his side of the big double bed, where the nubbly white chenille spread hung neatly over the end. I walked to the foot of the bed and waited for him to tell Grandma to stop crying.

He didn't move.

I went over to wake him, touching his shoulder. He was cold and stiff.

It didn't occur to me to scream. Or to speak. I had energy for only one thing.

I turned and ran.

I ran faster than I had ever run from Wowser. Faster than in any of the games of Hide-and-Seek, Sardines, Tag, or Split. I ran out of the bedroom door, into the hall, and back to my own room where I jumped into the bed with Stevie. I wrapped myself around him, big spoon around little spoon, and listened to his little *pop-pop-pop* snores till Mommy came in and told us both that Grandpa Dan was gone.

"Gone?" Stevie asked. "Gone where? Can we go with him?"

Stevie didn't understand what she meant. But I knew. I had known it the minute I touched him.

Gone. Not like Daddy who was *gone* overseas. Not *gone* like us from New York.

Gone. Like in dead. No more stories. No more tree house. No more cut curls.

Gone. Like in forever.

Grandma cried in her bedroom for nearly a month. Mommy brought her meals up there, sat with her, tried to reason her back to herself. Aunt Cecily came over and tried the same. But Grandma had to cry that sorrow out, I guess. There was so much in her, I couldn't imagine it all.

Stevie would sometimes go and sit on her lap and they would rock together for a long time in silence, staring out of the window till he got bored and left.

But I couldn't bring myself to cross the threshold of the bedroom. I would stand in the hall and call out, "Grandma, please. Please, Grandma." Until one day she saw me standing there, and stood up, smiling.

"I think we need to make some applesauce," she said.

I followed her like a little shadow down the back stairs. That day I chopped apples in the wooden bowl till my hand was sore. But I wouldn't stop, afraid—I think—that only my chopping kept her in the kitchen, kept her out of the crying room.

I never went into the long closet again.

✦　✦　✦

Notes from Jane Yolen

"My father's family, the Yolens, are liars, but more politely call themselves storytellers. If it's a choice between what really happened and what makes a better story, they go for story every time.

My mother's family, the Berlins, always tell the truth. Except about important things. Like age. Like death.

I guess I am a bit of both.

But all families have stories that change and grow over the years. Stories that start with a kernel of truth and get bigger. My own children stand behind my back when I tell these kind of stories, making their fingers into quotation marks and whispering to anyone who is listening, 'Author Embellishment.'

So I suppose the story of the long closet, a Berlin story told by a Yolen, has been embellished by time and by memory. What I have written is how I remember the story of my grandfather's death, except that I couldn't recall Wowser's real name and so had to make that up. And I couldn't recall the other games we played as children, so I made that part up, too. And while I remember Grandma's flowered housedresses vividly, as well as the fox stole and the crepe dress, the rest of what was in the long closet is pretty hazy.

I called my Aunt Cecily after I finished writing this

story. 'Tell me,' I asked, 'what really happened the night Grandpa died.' Interesting that in fifty years I had never asked that particular question.

She said Grandpa had been working hard at the store. He came home, lay down in bed, had a massive heart attack, and died. He was fifty-four years old, younger than I am right now. 'If you kids and your mother hadn't been living there,' Aunt Cecily added, 'I do believe Grandma would have died, too. She would have mourned herself to death.'

For years after Grandpa died, my mother tried to write stories. But she was a Berlin, not a Yolen. Stories to her were just lies. She felt that they had to be entirely made up, and so she did not put the truth in any of them. She sold only one story in her lifetime, to *Reader's Digest*, a piece that she wrote with a friend under the pseudonym Yolanda Field about not being able to have children and then—miraculously—having twins. My father, on the other hand, wrote magazine and newspaper stories that had only a nodding acquaintance to reality. He made up 'facts' with abandon, but was always, somehow, true to the core of what he was reporting.

Luckily, I got the Yolen genes in good number and I tell tales that are true, not true, and somewhere in between.

Author embellishment indeed!"

✦   ✦   ✦

Left to right:
Elaine* - Sherry - Harriett

E.L. Konigsburg

❖ ❖ ❖

How I Lost My Station in Life

◆

E. L. KONIGSBURG

Except for the time I want to tell about, the year and a half when we lived in Youngstown, Ohio, we always lived over the store. When my father managed Harris's Men's Clothiers in Phoenixville, Pennsylvania, we did, and then when he went into business for himself and opened a ladies' dresses and dry goods store just two blocks down the street, we did again.

Living over the store had its advantages. For one thing, we were always downtown, and every important thing was nearby. As soon as I was allowed to cross the street by myself (look both ways, even after waiting for the light on the corner to change) I could walk to school, to the library, to Sunday school, and I could walk to the Colonial for the Saturday movie matinee with my sister Harriett—two Ts.

Harriett and I shared a bedroom at our new place

over the store. A door in our bedroom led to a little balcony that hung over the narrow space between our building and Troxell's Jewelry Store next door. We had orders not to set foot on it. It was not safe. So there it was, as romantic as Juliet's balcony when she was wooed by Romeo and as useful as a hangnail. I didn't mind too much. I was a basic indoor child. I had my reasons.

I was not very good at sports.

Awkward would be a kind term.

Clumsy would be accurate.

The sidewalk was our playground. I was not good at any of the sidewalk games. *Hopscotch:* Drew the lines better than I could stay off them. *Jump rope:* Never could jump in. Always had to stand in. (Double dutch is still a mystery.) *Roller-skating:* Fell a lot. Never learned to brake. Had to run into something to stop myself. *Bicycling:* Still bear a scar under my chin from when I finally learned to ride a two-wheeler and went straight into a fire hydrant.

I was also hopeless at music. Once a week Miss Klinger came into our classroom to teach us music. She divided our class into redbirds and bluebirds. The bluebirds were allowed to sing; the redbirds listened. I was a redbird. At Christmas redbirds were allowed to sing, but all Miss Klinger offered were carols. Being

Jewish, I did not think I should, but I wanted to, so I did. But I never sang all the words. When I came to Jesus or Christ, I hummed.

Fortunately, gym and music were never given letter grades. (How could anyone give a redbird a grade when she was never allowed to sing?) So those subjects never interfered with one of my two best things: Getting As. My other best thing was being the baby of the family.

Although there were occasions, like music days, when I did not enjoy school, I always enjoyed—really, really enjoyed—being the baby of the family. There were only two of us. Although Harriett was smart and responsible, these things were expected of her, for she was the older sister. The baby of the family is never expected to do things as well as the older ones do—and when you are the baby of the family, they are all the older ones. The baby of the family is always in training. She gets the kind of attention that is something between being a daughter and being a household pet. And she feels slightly adorable even when she isn't. There is an *unexpected* quality to everything you do when you are the baby of the family.

Phoenixville was a mill town. The mill was called Ajax. I don't know what was manufactured there, but I do know that when the mill closed down, people stopped buying dresses and dry goods. My parents had to close up shop, and we had to move from over the store.

I was in the middle of fifth grade. I was in the middle of learning about decimals in math and in the middle of learning about the middle of Europe in geography. Before we left, my school principal gave my mother two envelopes for my new school principal. One had my school records and the other had a "To Whom It May Concern" letter. My mother never let me see that letter because it contained my IQ and standard test scores, which were big secrets back then, especially to the person whom they most concerned— me. I had overheard my mother and father whispering about that letter, and I knew they were proud of whatever it said.

We packed up the family Plymouth four-door and went west, all across the width of Pennsylvania, and moved in with Aunt Rozella in Youngstown, Ohio.

Compared to Phoenixville, Youngstown was big. Last year's geography book printed **Youngstown** in boldface and gave it four lines of text. Phoenixville was not even mentioned.

Compared to our place over the store, Aunt Rozella's house was big. Aunt Rozella's husband was so successful that I was sure that if he ever appeared in a textbook, **Uncle Iz** would be printed in boldface and be given at least four lines.

Although this was to be only a temporary arrangement until we could find affordable housing, I think my mother did not like being beholden to her younger sister; and I think having a whole family move in must have felt like a minor invasion to Aunt Ro. She had a big house, yes, but she had her own uses for it. There was Aunt Ro herself, **Uncle Iz**, Dorothy, their live-in maid, and their adorable little boy, my cousin Morley. Morley was smart for his age—not smart enough to get As in school, but only because he was too young to go.

Except for Morley, who paid attention to no one, and my father, who was on the road in the Plymouth four-door, none of us was very comfortable during the week in Aunt Ro's big house with the live-in maid.

Weekends were another matter. On weekends we went to Farrell, just over the state line in Pennsylvania, where my father would meet us. There we stayed with my father's sister. Aunt Wilma worked in a bakery, and she lived over the store, and her children—she had two—were older than I was, older than Harriett, and one of them was old enough to drive us from Youngstown to Farrell. At Aunt Wilma's we were much more crowded and much more comfortable.

But on Mondays it was back to Youngstown.

Right across the street from Aunt Rozella's house was Warren G. Harding Elementary School, and a few blocks farther on was Rayen High, the only public high school on the entire Northside. A lot of kids from lesser neighborhoods went there. Harriett registered at Rayen. Once enrolled, she could remain there even after we found affordable housing.

Warren G. Harding Elementary School, on the other hand, did not have kids from lesser neighborhoods; so when my mother marched across the street to register me for the fifth grade, she knew that I would not be there when we moved into our affordable housing in a lesser neighborhood. I would be there for a few weeks at most. It was the time of year between the end of Christmas break and the start of a new semester, and both Mom and Dad had promised that by the start of the new semester, we would leave Aunt Ro's. So even though my mother knew that going to Harding would be a temporary thing, she took that "To Whom It May Concern" letter over to the principal and enrolled me in their fifth grade.

By this time I had observed that my cousin Morley, who paid attention to no one, needed a lot of attention himself. Furthermore, whenever attention was to be paid, he always needed to be the center of it. I had also observed that as adorable as he was, when Morley didn't get his way, he was not. Furthermore, as the new family pet, he was treated as extremely adorable even when he wasn't even slightly.

As long as we lived at Aunt Ro's, I would be expected to do things as well as the older ones—because I was one of them now. As long as we lived at Aunt Ro's, I would have to make do with only one of my two best things; and that was getting As.

But there was a problem. Fifth grade at Warren G. Harding Elementary School was not in the middle of the middle of Europe in geography. They were in the middle of the United States. And, within the first week of my being there, they would be having a semester test. I was determined to pass that test, and not only pass it, but get an A. Maybe an A—plus.

I had to. I had to show everyone, Aunt Rozella and Uncle Iz—and most especially me, myself—that I could do what was expected—whatever that "To Whom It May Concern" letter had said I could.

When I got my A—maybe an A—plus—my new principal could announce it over the public-address system that, against all odds, Elaine Lobl had gotten an A—maybe an A—plus—on the semester test in geography. And when I walked into the classroom, the new teacher and all the students could give me a standing ovation—whatever that was.

I crammed. I made my mother ask me every question at the end of every chapter. I practiced spelling the names of all the cities I was to know about, and when I went to bed, the only thing that kept me from having nightmares was the dream of that teacher leading the applause as I went up to collect my perfect paper.

She passed out the corrected test papers, starting with the highest score. Not mine. Second highest, not mine. Third, not mine. I was about two-thirds of the way down the list. (I still remember one of the questions: What is the chief food fed to pigs in Virginia? I didn't know the answer then, but I do now.)

When you have lost your home, when you have a "To Whom It May Concern" letter to live up to, when you are no longer the baby of the family, when you think that getting an unexpected A is all you can do to restore your place in the family, being two-thirds down the list is as good as failure.

I carried my test paper across the street. Aunt Ro asked me how I did, and swallowing hard, I answered, "She asked the wrong questions for the answers I gave."

Finally, we had a house to rent. And not a minute too soon. I was happy to leave Aunt Ro, Cousin Morley, and Warren G. Harding: Displaced, replaced, and out of place.

A new semester was starting, and I would be going

to William McKinley Elementary School. My teacher would be Miss Frances Thompson, and neither she nor the principal, Mr. Perkins, would see the "To Whom It May Concern" letter because I begged my mother not to show it to them.

William McKinley Elementary did not have a lunchroom. My dad was still looking for work, selling notions out of the back of his car to make expenses, so he did not come home during the week and certainly not for lunch. My sister was at Rayen High, which had a school cafeteria, so she did not come home for lunch either. I did. It was just Mama and just me. Just canned soup and good rye bread. We were as poor as we would ever be, but those lunch hours were rich magic. My mother would have lunch on the table and the radio on our favorite soap opera when I came home. We would listen to *Mary Noble, Backstage Wife* while we ate lunch, and then we would redd up and talk. ("Redd up" is what Pennsylvanians say instead of "tidying up.")

My mother and I loved the same radio programs and Franklin D. Roosevelt. We loved the same movie stars and hated the same ones, too. We both loved clothes but couldn't afford any. My mother seemed to want for me exactly the same things I wanted for myself. She was proud of me, and I was proud of her. I thought my mother was perfect, and she made me feel that I was almost. We had a kind of easiness with each other, and I couldn't think of living anywhere that she was not. I loved her achingly.

When Miss Thompson passed out report cards for that first six weeks' grading period, she announced that she was giving out the best report card she had ever made out in all her years of teaching: All As and one A—minus. And that report card was mine. I was back where I belonged—at the head of the class at William McKinley Elementary School and the baby of the family at 1507 Florencedale Avenue.

When I got to sixth grade, I had two new teachers, Mrs. Clark and Miss Mayer, both of whom I loved— although I probably loved Mrs. Clark more. I was getting As from both of them, and I was sometimes allowed to sing even when it wasn't Christmas.

Then a few months before my eleventh birthday, on a day that will go down in infamy, my mother announced that she was going to have a baby. My mother, who would not even consider letting us have a puppy because we couldn't afford another mouth to feed, this same mother announced that she was about to have a baby.

I was to be replaced again. I was outraged.

And I was embarrassed. By then, I knew what it took to get pregnant, and I thought that my mother ought to be ashamed of herself, that at her age—she was thirty-four years old—she had done it.

Neither my father nor my mother ever used the word *pregnant*. He said that my mother "was in the family way," and she said that she "was expecting."

My father was still having a lot of trouble finding steady work, still traveling, still coming home only on the odd weekend, and I suspected that he was no more pleased than I was about having a new baby in the family, but I supposed he felt partly responsible. My father asked Harriett and me to take care of her. Knowing how responsible Harriett was, he asked her to arrange to double up on her classes so that when the semester was over, she could skip the rest of the school year and stay home to take care of our mother. Harriett agreed.

Only weeks later, I was told that we couldn't pay the rent at 1507 Florencedale. I was told that we would be moving to cheaper housing in a lesser neighborhood. Still Youngstown. Still the Northside. Still Rayen High for Harriett. But not William McKinley for me. Our new place would be in a different elementary school district. I was to be displaced again.

Mr. Perkins, the school principal, called my

mother in to school and told her that he and both my teachers, Miss Mayer and Mrs. Clark, thought I would be out of place at the new school. They wanted me to stay at William McKinley, and if my mother would allow me to be bused, they could get an out-of-district permission for me. She agreed.

So every morning, Harriett and I caught a city bus, using school bus coupons. I got off at the Thornton Street stop on Fifth Avenue and walked the few blocks to the big yellow brick building that said "McKinley School" carved in stone above the door. Harriett rode on to Rayen High. I carried my lunch and ate alone in Mrs. Clark's classroom.

When her doubling-up semester was over, it was Harriett who had those magic lunch hours with my mother. I was left out.

I no longer thought that my mother was perfect, and she no longer made me feel that I was almost.

I helped with the supper dishes, and I learned to help with the ironing, but I still felt left out. I felt as if I had not only lost my lunch companion, I had lost my place at the table. We no longer had a kind of easiness with each other, I began to think of my mother as "She."

She who was expecting was not feeling too healthy most of the time. She developed a terrible rash on her arms and chest, and her gums bled when she brushed her teeth. She was anemic even though she had the appetite of a sumo wrestler. She craved strange foods out of season. Every time she had to stand for any length of time, the veins in her legs swelled and turned blue, and as her stomach grew, so did the size and number of blue swollen veins. The veins had a name: *Varicose,* but my mother was a *She,* and the baby was an *it.* Not even a capital *i.* Just *it.*

Harriett and I walked with her to Dr. Kaufmann's office downtown because we didn't have money for bus fare. Our new apartment was closer to town than Florencedale Avenue had been, but since we lived on the second floor, she who was in the family way did a lot of huffing and puffing getting up that flight of stairs. We had no health insurance, and Medicaid had not yet been invented, and we had neither friends nor family in the medical profession, so Dr. Kaufmann agreed to deliver it at a lowered fee because he was Aunt Rozella's doctor and personal friend, a fact she reminded us of even though Dr. Kaufmann didn't.

My father found a job in Farrell. And he found us affordable housing. As soon as school was over, we would once again be living over a store. We would have a kitchen downstairs and a living room, two bed-rooms, and a bath upstairs—over the store. The store itself was empty. The windows were not boarded up, but were whited out with a paste made from Bon Ami cleanser.

We had hardly moved our furniture into the new place when my father said, "her time is near," and we had to move her back to Aunt Rozella's so that she could be near the hospital and Dr. Kaufmann.

I thought to myself, "It better be a boy." A baby brother would allow me to be The Baby Sister, a secondary role, but one that would certainly have more status than being The Middle Child.

She delivered it on June 12, right on schedule.

It was a girl.

She named it Sherry Hope.

She actually thought that she had invented the name Sherry.

I found out that she was nursing it instead of giving it a bottle, and that was just more proof of how she was just too old and too old-fashioned to be having babies. To myself, I called it Sherry Hope-There's-No-More.

Back then, Southside Hospital in Youngstown, Ohio, kept women who had just given birth for two full weeks, and they would not allow anyone under the age of fourteen to set foot inside. So Harriett, who was fifteen and a half, got to see it, and so did Aunt Rozella.

Uncle Iz could have gone if he had wanted to. Even Aunt Ruth was allowed to go. Aunt Ruth was about to have a baby herself, but Southside let her in regardless of what she might be carrying. Not me. They wouldn't let me see it. Everyone who did said that it was as beautiful as its name.

Since Dad's new job meant that he had regular working hours, he went every night, and guess who he took along with him? Harriett, his fifteen-and-a-half-year-old daughter. He told me that even though he, too, had wanted a boy, he had to admit that it was beautiful.

So on the fifteenth day after it was born, Harriett and my father went to the hospital to bring them home. I had to stay behind to redd up the house. I waited by the window until I saw the car pull up. I was outside by the curb waiting when she stepped out of the family Plymouth and handed me a bundle in a pink flannel receiving blanket. She told me to support its neck.

I pulled the blanket back.

And I saw.

I saw the most beautiful baby in the whole world. A gorgeous, golden baby girl.

This was no "it." This was Sherry. Sherry Hope Lobl. This was my baby sister, as bright and as golden as the wine of her name.

From that moment on, I didn't want to let her go, and I never have. The new baby of the family became the girl who is my sister who became the woman who is my lifelong friend.

Sherry and I are both grandmothers now. She lives in southern Ohio, and I live in north Florida, but we talk to each other on the phone every day—sometimes a couple of times a day—and we have the phone bills to prove it.

✦   ✦   ✦

Notes from E. L. Konigsburg

"In those Youngstown days when my father was out of work and trying so hard to find a job, I didn't know that what was happening to our family was happening to a lot of other families, too. That period of history is so famous that it has a name: The Great Depression.

When I was your age, the only way I could relate to the world at large was by reading books, but what I found there never matched what I saw around me. If the kids were poor, they lived in England a long time ago. If they had adventures, they didn't live in land-locked places like Farrell, Pennsylvania, or Youngstown, Ohio. And if their mothers were having babies, no one mentioned varicose veins or children who felt they were being replaced.

I was a grown woman and a mother of three before I even thought about becoming a writer. After the third of my three children started kindergarten, I decided to write. I was prompted to do so more by incidents that happened in their lives than by incidents that happened in mine. I wanted to write something that reflected their kind of growing up because when I was your age, I never felt that the books I read reflected me.

My sister Harriett lived in Farrell until last year, when she moved to nearby Hermitage. Both of her married children live near Youngstown.

I don't think you would call my cousin Morley cute now, but you would call him handsome. He is still smart for his age. He is a **federal judge** in Ohio.

The yellow brick building that was William McKinley Elementary School is boarded up, and the little patch of yard around it is littered and unkempt. Towns change. Memories don't. In my mind, those yellow bricks are golden."

✦　✦　✦

Howard Norman

* * *

Bus Problems

✦

HOWARD NORMAN

In the summer of 1959, I spent every weekday as an assistant to Mr. Pinnie Oler, librarian and driver of the bookmobile. This was in Grand Rapids, Michigan. It was a very hot summer. In fact, on the day I want especially to tell about, July 23, WGRD radio announced that it was the hottest day of the decade so far: 103°.

The bookmobile was an old, rickety school bus painted blue. It was fitted inside with bookshelves and two leather benches you could sit on to read. The benches were repaired with small strips of masking tape. There was a fan screwed to the dashboard, and a second fan was nailed to the back shelves, so that air circulated nicely and helped cool things down.

Mr. Oler was, I would guess, about forty. He had a slight Dutch accent. There were a lot of Dutch Reform churches in town. He was about five feet eight inches tall, the same height as my father. Mr. Oler had a thin face, a sad face, I thought. He had sandy brown hair combed straight back. He always wore tan-colored slacks, white socks, black high-topped tennis shoes and a long-sleeved white shirt. He *never* rolled up the sleeves, not even on the hottest day of the 1950s.

In the *Grand Rapids Press*, the job had been listed as a "volunteer position." The day after school got out, June 9, my mother, Estelle, took me to the book-mobile and said, "My son's interested in the job." After shaking my hand and scarcely looking me over, Mr. Oler said, "He'll do fine." I started work the very next morning. My job included repairing torn pages with Scotch tape, spraying books with a special solution that killed dust mites, writing out overdue notices, and other odds and ends. From the get-go, I took my job seriously. When I stepped into the bookmobile at 8:45 on the corner of Giddings and Market Street, Mr. Oler would say, "Good morning, kid," then hand me a list of chores. Also, he kept an ice chest near his seat and gave me a bottle of Ne-Hi orange soda to go with my lunch every noon. Actually, in the Midwest we called it "pop," not soda. I remember this job as being the first thing I was truly proud of.

I had only one friend—one was enough. His name was Paul Amundson. I would have hung out with Paul after work and on weekends, no doubt about it, but that summer he was visiting his grandparents in Norway. I wrote him a letter:

Dear Paul,

I'm working on the bookmobile this summer.
See you this September.

Your friend,
Howard

It was the first letter I ever wrote. A few weeks later, I got Paul's return postcard from Norway; it had a stamp showing the head and antlers of a reindeer.

Let us say that you were standing next to the driver's seat of the bookmobile and facing the back. Filling the right-side top three shelves were books about zoology, astronomy, medicine, all under the category of SCIENCE. The bottom three shelves held GOVERNMENT/SOCIAL SCIENCE. The shelves along the back wall contained SPORTS/RECRE-ATION/HOBBIES. Now, along the left side of the bookmobile: the top three shelves held FICTION/POETRY, whereas the bottom three were reserved for children's books, under the sign that said JUVENILE. The wooden card catalogue was in the back left corner. On top of the catalogue was a slotted box: BOOK REQUESTS.

The bookmobile was a secure and peaceful place.

My father was away somewhere mysterious and unknown to me that summer. He was what I would call a ghost in our house, someone who once belonged but no longer did, yet insisted on showing up now and then, causing a disturbance, getting everyone upset, then disappearing to who knows where. I had three brothers. My older brother was at a disciplinary camp for juvenile delinquents; he had stolen a car. My two younger brothers were at home with my mother. I was happy to not spend my days at home. All in all, the bookmobile gave me a lot of privacy. And I had ample time to carry out my most private passion, which was looking at photographs (in the SCIENCE section) and reading (in SCIENCE and FICTION) about the Arctic—the most remote and barren region of the world. Eskimos, polar bears, icebergs. In the book-mobile I read all the books written by Jack London. *White Fang* was my favorite. From such novels I understood that the far north was a place where serious once-in-a-lifetime adventures were taking place. Though I also remember thinking that if I lived in the Arctic I would miss trees. I loved the big shady maple and oak trees in Michigan.

Like any kid footloose on the weekends, I more or less killed time. I rode my bicycle. I fished for crappies and sunfish in Reed's Lake and the Thornapple River. But the bookmobile was my weekday home that summer.

Engine-wise, the bus was dilapidated, and often broke down. Mr. Oler would just shrug and say, "We've got a bus problem." The bus might stall out in the middle of the street, the radiator might spout steam and water like a geyser, or oil might spill out beneath the bus. When we had a bus problem, Mr. Oler would find the nearest telephone and call his wife, Martha, who was a mechanic for the Grand Rapids school system.

Martha Oler was a very beautiful woman. I'd guess she was at least ten years younger than Mr. Oler. I saw her about five times that summer. I thought that she looked confident and interesting in her mechanic's overalls. When she pulled up in her pickup truck, Mr. Oler was always happy to see her. She would park the truck and carry her toolbox to the bookmobile. But before looking at the engine, she always kissed Mr. Oler. I mean, they took a long moment to hold and kiss each other. Martha Oler had dark red hair and was an inch or so taller than Mr. Oler. She had a quick smile.

Whenever she came to fix the bookmobile, she poked her head inside and said, "Fancy seeing you here!" Which of course was a little joke, since I was *always* on the bookmobile. A couple of times she could not fix the bus problem and had to call a tow truck. Waiting for the tow, she and Mr. Oler would hold hands, lean against her truck, and talk. Mr. Oler would pop open a Ne-Hi orange and share it with his wife without wiping the rim on his sleeve, the way us kids were taught to do.

Besides stops for bus problems, there were what Mr. Oler called "unscheduled stops." He was truthful with me about this. "Howard," he said, the first time he parked the bus in front of his and Martha's apartment in the middle of an afternoon, "I'm making an unscheduled stop. My wife and I are trying to have a baby." That is all he said or needed to say. I was too young to think about it in any detail. I only knew that he and Martha needed to see each other privately. At such times, Mr. Oler carried out the same routine. He would step out of the bookmobile, pop open the hood as if the radiator had boiled over, then disappear inside his apartment building. I would keep myself busy.

And so it was, on July 23 at about 3:00 P.M., that Mr. Oler made an unscheduled stop. He propped open the hood and went into his building. Using a world atlas open on my lap as a table, I wrote out the overdue notices. But it was no more than five minutes after Mr. Oler had gone inside that a surprise visitor stepped on board. I recognized Tommy Allen right away. He was what my mother called a "JD," which stood for Juvenile Delinquent. Still, she fed him supper three or four nights a week. I had seen a magazine photograph of Sal Mineo in the movie *Rebel Without A Cause,* and had heard my brother and Tommy call the actor "very cool." I think Tommy modeled his look after Sal Mineo: slicked-back black hair, black jeans, black tee shirt. He was my older brother's best friend.

When he got inside the bookmobile, he said, "I was walking to downtown. I see the hood's up. You got a breakdown?"

"Yeah. Mr. Oler had to make a phone call," I said, trying to protect Mr. Oler's privacy, since the truth was none of Tommy's business, I felt. "He's in his apartment. He'll be out pretty soon."

"That's convenient, the bus breaking down in front of his apartment," Tommy said. "Oh well. I'll just wait here with you. Maybe Pinnie Oler'd give me a lift toward downtown a ways. It's a scorcher out, ain't it?"

"Hottest day of the decade."

"Says who?" Tommy said.

"Says WGRD."

"WGRD," Tommy said, "oh, well, then. Sure it's true."

"Can you really cook an egg on the sidewalk on a day like this?" I said.

"I cooked one this morning," Tommy said. "Right out in front of my house."

"I wish I could've seen that," I said. "What'd you do with the egg?"

"I ate it, dummy," Tommy said. "If it's this hot tomorrow, come on by. I'll cook one on the sidewalk for you."

I looked out the window and saw a young woman, about age fifteen, riding her bicycle across the field opposite the apartment building. As she got closer, I could see that she wore a one-piece black bathing suit with a short-sleeved white shirt over it, and flip-flop sandals. She had a fancy new-looking bicycle. She rode right up to the bookmobile, got off her bike, opened the kickstand, propped up the bicycle, and stepped into the bookmobile. She was about Tommy's height. She had dark brown hair; you could see comb tracks in it. Tommy took one look at her and said, "Hello, baby," but he said it in a fake television-actor kind of way, I thought.

"Baby, baby, baby, *wah wah wah*," the young woman said, as though she was a baby in a crib. "Do I look like a *baby* to you?"

"No, I guess not," Tommy said.

Things happened in a strange and quick order now. She took out a comb from her shirt pocket, stood in front of the rear-view mirror above the driver's seat, crouched a bit, and combed her hair. Then she turned and said, "What are you boys doing inside on a day like this? Just across the field's a pond. Nobody else is there. Oh; my mom would kill me if she knew I went swimming with two boys and no lifeguard around. She'd be so mad."

But I don't think Tommy heard past the word "pond." A look of horror crossed his face.

The pond the girl had spoken of was known in our neighborhood as the "polio pond." It was a small pond at a gravel quarry gouged out of a vast rocky field. The quarry was about a quarter-mile from Mr. and Mrs. Oler's apartment. Anyway, this was a time in which polio, a really frightening disease that paralyzed you, was on everyone's mind. Staring out from posters all over town were a lame boy and a lame girl, both on crutches. The posters were designed to raise money to fight polio. In *Life* magazine I'd seen pictures of a girl who had to spend her childhood trapped inside an iron lung in a special hospital.

In our neighborhood, rumor had it that you could catch polio from getting even one single drop of the polio pond in your mouth. I don't know how such a stupid and false rumor got started and then became a more powerful truth than real truth, but I believed this rumor with all my heart. I knew that Tommy and my older brother believed it, too, because they had a curse, "I hope you fall into the polio pond!" which they used only on their worst enemies. True, the pond *looked* normal. It was very pleasant looking, actually, with frogs and tadpoles and cattails waving along the edges, and lily pads. But hidden in its waters was polio, and God help the person who dared swim or fish or even dip a toe in that pond.

". . . pond . . ." said the girl, and Tommy was fast out the bookmobile door.

He ran to the front and slammed down the hood. Then he raced back inside, sat in the driver's seat, turned the key in the ignition, started up the engine, and yelled back at me, "A breakdown, huh? You lied to me!" He shifted gears, and we hurtled forward. The bus jerked a few times, but Tommy was handy with vehicles—my brother had called him "a genius with cars"—and he quickly got the hang of driving the bus.

"Hey, what're you doing?" the young woman shouted, and then broke into a nervous laugh.

"Getting you to the hospital!" Tommy shouted, then concentrated on the road.

I threw myself onto a reading bench and hung on for dear life.

"You idiot!" the girl screamed at Tommy. "My new bike's back there!"

Blodgett Memorial Hospital was only five or six blocks away. Tommy pulled up to the EMERGENCY entrance. He turned off the ignition, yanked up the emergency brake, opened the door, and ran inside. In a minute he returned with two attendants, a nurse, and a doctor. They all piled into the bookmobile. By this time the girl was standing straight-backed against the card catalogue. "There she is," Tommy said, pointing.

"What seems to be the trouble with her?" the doctor asked Tommy in a very gruff, doubting voice.

"She . . . she . . . she swam in a pond that's got polio germs in it. The quarry pond. She's probably caught it."

The doctor's face stiffened and he looked furious. "There's nothing wrong with that girl, is there? This hospital, son, is *not* a place for practical jokes. Polio is not a practical joke." Without another word, he nodded to the two attendants, who grabbed Tommy and me and took us into the hospital. The nurse escorted the young woman from the bookmobile. She was laughing and crying. Inside a room marked SECURITY we were watched over by an attendant.

Two policemen soon arrived. They took down our names and telephone numbers. Then they went out into the hallway to consult with each other. One policeman came back and said, "Okay, you and you,"—he pointed to me and the young woman— "my partner's calling your parents to come and get each of you. You,"—he pointed to Tommy—"you come with me." Tommy followed the policeman out to the police car.

In the hour or so that we waited in the room, the girl only said, "My name is Marcia."

When I got home, I told my mother the whole story.

A few weeks later, we all met again in a court-room. My mother stood next to me. Tommy's uncle Will stood with him. Marcia had both of her parents with her. The judge said, "Now, Mr. Thomas Allen, for the offenses listed here today, you could be charged as an adult. You don't, however, have any previous record. And your uncle suggests there was actually a rea-son *why* you stole a bookmobile, and then foisted some far-fetched story having to do with"—the judge looked at his notes—"*polio* to the emergency-room doctor. What in the world possessed you to concoct such a tall tale, Mr. Allen?"

Tommy's uncle pressed Tommy's lower back with his hand, making Tommy stand in a respectful, upright posture. "Well," Tommy said, "this girl rode up on her bicycle. She said she'd been swimming in the polio pond."

"Which you actually believe threatened Marcia's life?" the judge said.

"Yes, I did believe it," Tommy said.

"And *still* believe it?" the judge said, shaking his head slowly back and forth, as if suggesting that Tommy say "No."

Tommy looked at Marcia.

"If you swim in that pond, you definitely could catch polio," Tommy said. "Marcia, there, swam in it, and I think you should order her to have a checkup, just in case."

"I see," the judge said. "Well, stupidity and good intentions notwithstanding, I am sentencing you, Mr. Allen, to sixty days at the Kent County Camp for Delinquents. It's not jail, mind you. It could have been jail."

"Thank you, your honor," Tommy's uncle said.

Tommy's uncle pressed Tommy's back hard. "Yes, thank you, your honor," Tommy said, half mumbling.

"And as for you, Mr. Norman," the judge said. "You should not have been left alone on the bookmobile in the first place. I have already reprimanded Mr. Oler for such an oversight. Mr. Oler and I have settled this matter. I hope your mother's already given you a good talking-to, as well."

The judge struck his gavel. As the court officer led him from the room, Tommy turned and gave me a nice, forgiving smile, which I thought was the most generous thing anyone had ever done for me. He was forgiving me, I felt, for not shouting out, "He tried to save the girl's life!" Because I knew that was the truth.

I was allowed to go back to work on the book-mobile. Mr. Oler never mentioned the incident to me. I never mentioned it to him, either. Later, I heard that the place they sent Tommy to was a farm about twenty minutes south of Grand Rapids. Tommy had to slop pigs and feed cows and chickens, and rake out a barn. I heard that he wore his black tee shirt, black jeans, and black shoes every day. Plus, he wore sunglasses, even in the farmhouse at night. It is true that he took the tractor out for a spin when he was not supposed to even touch it. They added a week onto his sentence for that. I also heard that everyone at the correctional farm got to like him a lot.

Mr. and Mrs. Oler had a baby girl.

✦ ✦ ✦

Notes from Howard Norman

"I chose this particular story to tell because I really never forgave myself for not speaking up in court that day, and because I feel that sometimes life just sparks moments of great drama. Such moments haunt you, and if you can detail and animate them on paper in a way that emboldens and honors the memory, you have become a writer. I never much wanted to write about my childhood, though I like to tell stories of what happened when I was young, especially to my daughter Emma, who is always saying, 'Okay, tell me what happened to you when you were——,' and then picks an age. In the case of 'Bus Problems,' what I wanted most to do was show how one minute day-to-day life can be so familiar, and then suddenly everything changes! Also, I wanted to write about Tommy Allen, who more than any TV or movie character, was a real 'action hero.'"

✦ ✦ ✦

michael g. moon

◆ ◆ ◆

Pegasus for a Summer

✦

MICHAEL J. ROSEN

This is a true story about a horse. It's also a mostly true story about the horse's rider, me, but I can hardly distinguish what I remember from what I'd *like* to remember—or to forget—about myself the summer that ended as I entered seventh grade.

Outside school, I did two things better than most kids (and doing better probably meant as much to me as it meant to everyone else): swimming and horseback riding. Yet without a pool or a stable at school, I could never prove those talents to anyone. But the day camp I attended each summer provided for both.

Oh, one year, I did compete on a swim team with my best friend Johnny. I swallowed a teaspoon of honey-energy before each event with the others in my relay. All season, my eyes bore raccoon rings from the goggles. Ribbons hung from my bedroom corkboard.

But I hated it, hated it just as I hated every sport that had fathers barking advice from the sidelines, or hot-shot classmates divvying the rest of us into shirts and skins, or coaches always substituting in their favorite players, and team members who knew every spiteful name for someone who missed a catch, overshot a goal, slipped out of bounds, fouled, fumbled, or failed them personally in any of a zillion ways.

But I didn't give up swimming, as I had baseball, football, and basketball. (Their seasons were so brief, how could a person master one skill before everyone switched to the next sport?) And I devoted myself to horseback riding.

The whole idea of camp, which represented the whole idea of summer, hinged on those few hours each week at the camp stable, just as the whole of the school year merely anticipated the coming summer vacation. At camp, it was simply me against—against no one. It was me *with* the horse. The two of us composed the entire team, and we competed with greater opponents than just other kids. We outmaneuvered gravity, vanquished our separate fears, and mastered a third language: the wordless communication of touch and balance.

Still, I never completely lost my fear of this massive, nearly unknowable animal who was fifteen times my weight, and I don't know how many times my gawky human strength. "Keep in mind, the horse perceives *you* as the bigger animal," our riding instructor Ricki would always remind us, though not one of us believed her.

I had taken lessons from Ricki during five previous summer camps—how to read a horse's ear positions, conduct each movement with the reins, maintain posture and balance through each gait—yet the only thing I remember is that I loved riding. Maybe I loved it because I excelled. Maybe I excelled because I loved it. I'd climb in the saddle, and instantly, other riders, other horses in the ring, whatever it was I didn't want to do after camp or beginning in September at junior high—it all ceased to exist, along with the rest of my life on the ground, shrinking, fading behind the trail of dust the horse and I made heading to the horizon.

Curiously, most of the obnoxious kids, the ones who did the harassing and teasing during baseball or football practice, spent their hours on horseback jerking the reins to stop their horses from munching ground clover, or thumping their boots into the sides of their uninspired horses. Not that I deliberately rode circles around them, but . . .

On those Mondays, Wednesdays, and Fridays when we rode at camp, I insisted my mother pack carrots for my lunch (for my horse—I hated carrots). I pulled on long pants and boots even when the temperature soared into the nineties. I slipped dimes in my pocket just to buy a soda in the tack room after lessons. And most mornings, I bugged my favorite-counselor-of-all-time Mitch: Can I skip capture-the-flag and go help the younger kids saddle their horses? Can our group have our lunch at the stables? In short, can I exchange everything else camp offers for more time with the horses?

Since I was turning thirteen, this was my last summer of camp. Ricki allowed us, her senior riders, to choose our own horses. She guided us along the line of readied, haltered horses, describing each animal, hinting at its possible challenges:

"Now, Smoky, here—he's a Tennessee walker, pretty gentle, though a bit hard-mouthed. Good for one of you stronger boys. Maybe you, Allen?"

Mitch would nod in agreement, or look down the row for a more suitable match. He'd ridden most of the horses. He'd even owned a horse of his own before coming to Ohio for college.

Appaloosas, quarter horses, pintos, buckskins. Braided manes, palomino coats, legs with white stockings, faces marked with moons or stars—but really, personality was all that mattered: skittish, poky, docile, bullheaded, rascally, distracted. Some horses kicked when another horse came too close; some had to be neck-reined, others tightly reined; some wouldn't put up with a rider's mixed signals, and some, well, you couldn't always predict.

It was up to each of us to say how much spirit or obstinacy we could handle. Twenty-four riding sessions lay ahead. Almost seventy-five hours with that one chosen horse.

"Now Sparky's a girl who likes to move," Ricki said, as she swatted flies from another horse's eyes. "Used to be a jumper, too. Needs someone to keep her in check, who'd enjoy her spunk." Maybe because Ricki looked straight at me, remembering me from other summers; or maybe because of the horse's color (a flecked white coat that Ricki called "flea-bitten gray—and, no, that doesn't mean she has fleas"); or maybe because of Sparky's blue eyes that sparkled as the sun shined in (was that how she got her name?): whatever the reason, I walked right up and took Sparky's halter. Mitch gave me a quick pat on the back of my neck, which I took to be his approval.

For each riding session, we'd saddle and bridle our horses with the stable assistants' help, and then ride into the ring to practice figure eights, pivoting, cantering left and right—whatever maneuver Ricki had planned. Then it was out the gate and over a long plank bridge that spanned a marshy, spring-fed creek. As if walking a giant xylophone, the horses' hooves struck each board, and the hammered notes echoed through the hollow. Then, single file, we'd follow forest trails barely wider than a horse. Mitch would call over his shoulder to point out a horned owl's nest or the sort of tree from which baseball bats are made, or to warn us of an especially slippery embankment. Across hoof-muddied creeks, through shallow ravines, over rotting white pines and oaks, the horses performed almost without us. We simply leaned forward going under trees and backward heading down hills.

Eventually, we'd arrive at the meadow for "open practice," which mostly meant a chance to break loose. Though Ricki hadn't instructed us in any gait faster than a canter, some horses, Sparky included, just longed to gallop—it seemed more natural. Suddenly the *one, two and three, four* of her cantering hooves vanished into a lift-off, a levitation I could feel the way you can feel the instant a plane lifts off or a roller coaster dips, and I'd be weightless, hardly resting in the saddle, my heart clop-clopping its own rapid gait as I hovered at a velocity only the tears that the wind jerked from my eyes revealed. In those moments—how long did they last? No more than a minute or two— Sparky and I flew and the earth vanished entirely beneath us. She had become Pegasus, the winged Greek horse, and I, a twelve-year-old mortal, by some miracle, had been chosen to ride her.

And then, by accident, honestly, when we'd be

heading back toward the barn, some horses (Sparky included) would shift from a gallop to a dead run, which, of course, was absolutely forbidden. It was too uncontrolled, too dangerous even for us advanced kids. It was too risky to allow a charging horse to stampede into the yard, careening into the barn and startling the tethered horses and the bystanders. And it was too thrilling—countless times more thrilling than anything else I'd ever experienced—to stop.

Lessons ended inside the stables, heaving loose the impossibly heavy saddle, slipping out the grassy, frothy bit, brushing and carding the horse. It meant coming down to earth and I could clearly recognize the odors: the horse's short damp hair, scratchy wool saddle blankets, the warmed worn leather, sun-parched manure, sweet hay and oats.

And finally, before leaving, I took my own reward: a bottle of orange soda from the tack room cooler.

Sparky performed like no other horse I'd ever ridden. Even Ricki told my mother on parents' night, "Those two have a special rapport." At every session, I sensed improvement. Sparky's trot smoothed out, though that probably meant I was learning to settle into her stride. She understood the instant I reined, leaned, and thumped my heel to move us into a canter. With Sparky, I finally understood what Ricki meant about how the horse and rider work in such harmony that they merge powers and thoughts to become a single creature. On the other hand, almost every lesson Ricki would pull me aside to say something like, "The two of you ought to try a little more this or that." I knew that "the two of us" actually meant the one of me.

Every day of the July Fourth week, it thundershowered and lessons had to be held indoors. The horses liked this as little as we did, but even worse, the storm distracted them, unsettled them—Sparky's ears continually flicked forward and back, fixing on whatever the wind knocked, wherever the thunder cracked.

That Friday, riding our horses into the stalls, this one kid Brett let his appaloosa named Choco drink at the trough with two other horses, though Brett knew that crowding made his horse nervous. And sure enough, another horse nosed in, and Choco bolted backward, and started bucking. The nearby horses jolted away, whinnied, and toppled a cart of straw.

"Stop, you idiot son-of-a-bitch horse!" Brett shouted in panic. (While only the counselors minded the cussing, the horses, we all knew, did not like shouting.)

"Clear out," Mitch said, as he pulled campers from the area. "Brett! Quit screaming!"

Brett hunkered down, both hands clinging to the saddle horn, both feet flopping free of the stirrups. Then Choco's hooves fired into the stall door, knocking the gate from its hinges, and Brett toppled to the floor, wedged between the wall and his spooked horse.

Mitch snatched at Choco's whipping reins, which stopped the bucking for a moment. Ricki inched along the wall to help Brett slide out of the way. Mr. Olmstead, the stable owner, appeared, too, and seized Choco's bridle, while Ricki darted in to grab Brett. But then Choco reared, trying to yank his head free, and he did, his front legs boxing in the air. But since Mitch still tugged at the reins, Choco was off-balance and heaved himself backward, battering the rear of the stall, ramming his flank right into Ricki's chest, and pinning her momentarily against the wall.

And then there was screaming—whose? Brett's, no doubt, since he'd just missed being crushed. And probably everyone else's, too, as we crowded around. Ricki slumped to the straw floor as Mr. Olmstead and Mitch yanked Choco out of the barn.

Another counselor ran to call the ambulance. The stable hands hurried the horses into stalls or out into the field to make room for the medics. Mitch treated Ricki for shock—he draped a saddle blanket over her body and pulled bits of straw from her hair. Ricki squinted from the pain. Her mouth stayed open as though trying to get the air back into her lungs. I crouched beside her and talked in a low voice, repeating over and over—*everything will be all right, the ambulance is coming, just relax*—trying to keep her from nodding off. People were always doing that on television. Our bus idled right outside the door, ready to take us home. But we were going to be late. We had to wait, find out what was going to happen. A horse had hurt not just someone, but *Ricki*. We were in a different kind of shock.

A dazed weekend ended with Mitch's announcement at flag-raising, Monday morning. "It could have been much worse. That horse could have crushed more than a few ribs. She's got four broken ribs—did you know you don't wear a cast for ribs? But it also means no riding for Ricki, and probably no camp for her."

A few of us made Ricki cards or wrote letters. Mitch gave us her address and brought stamps to camp. It turned out that she lived on the same street as my grandmother, so I biked over three days that week to visit. There were always different cars in Ricki's driveway, so I'd ride over to Grandma's and have one of her ice-cream floats, then ride around the block a few more times, and then, convinced that Ricki was busy and didn't really want camp kids bothering her, race home for dinner. I also thought I'd tell my parents I wanted to stop going to camp; I circled that topic for three days as well, before dropping it.

The owner's youngest son, Gibby, took over for Ricki. We sort of knew him—he was the one who slapped the horses' rears to move them in or out of their stalls. Gibby didn't know our names. He didn't bother to use the horses' names. For three straight sessions, Gibby had us circle him in the ring while he pelted dirt clods at the horses that weren't keeping in step, until the time ran out.

Then someone besides us kids must have complained, because with only a few sessions left, Gibby brought out his own horse, Striker, told us to march behind him "in a perfectly straight line, one horse's-length apart," and led us to the meadow.

"You're on your own," he said. "Just don't run 'em." Then he dismounted and gathered dirt clods.

Mitch and I and a few other kids turned our horses away from the group, just as Gibby called out to someone, "Keep that blind mare to a trot." I leaned into a canter, and Sparky responded as though she, too, had been waiting for free practice. Behind us, Gibby shouted his warning again: "I said, don't race her. Take the field at a trot."

Just as I completed one half-circle, passing Mitch on his horse Paintbrush, a dirt clod whizzed past my chest. "You, for crying out loud! Listen to me!"

"You want me?" I called back as I jerked the reins to bring Sparky to a halt. Horses crisscrossed the field between Gibby and me.

"No, I want to talk to myself all day!" he shouted,

even though he'd come close enough to just talk. "Yes, you. Too many holes and burrows to be running a blind animal! Trot her. Got it? Trot."

"What do you mean? Sparky's not blind."

"Right. *She's* not blind, and *you're* not stupid. Look, kid, just keep it slow, got it?" And then Gibby turned to yell at another kid who'd dropped his reins over his horse's grazing head.

I hopped down and stood in front of Sparky. Her enormous eyes gazed to each side, blinking, wondering, no doubt, why we weren't flying, what I was doing on the ground. I moved to stare into her right eye, at the sun breaking from clouds that were as much in her eye as in the sky. And I shuffled over and stared into her left eye, at the herd of tiny horses and riders veering toward the woods. I pressed my face to her velvet muzzle, and I held my breath, trying not to cry, trying not to let my eyes water or my breath leak even a sob, but I couldn't. How many times had Sparky walked me through those woods, never once stumbling as she lifted her hooves across the gullies and rotting trees? She had always dodged slower horses and obstacles in the ring. She recognized me. Even Ricki said she did. A blind horse could do all that?

Before long, Mitch came to see what was wrong. I shook my head to answer his questions. *No,* I wasn't hurt. *No,* I wasn't scared. *No,* nothing happened. *No,* I'm not going to just hop on and ride on home. *No,* I don't care if the other kids see me crying. Ultimately, I said that I hated Gibby, I hated him, I hated camp, and everything else because how could I like anything if, if Sparky was blind! If the whole world was this unfair! Blind? How could I not have known that? Seen that? Felt that? Gibby was right: I was stupid—*and I was blind.*

I wanted to stand in that field and I wanted to cry at least until camp ended, and maybe until summer ended, and maybe until I turned thirteen or nineteen or thirty and this sadness, this overpoweringly sorry feeling—about Sparky, about myself—had run dry like the tears.

But it didn't take that long. The bus was waiting back at the stables. "Come on, I'll help you up," Mitch said and cupped his hands beside the stirrup as though I'd ever needed a boost from him or anyone else. I took Sparky's reins and led her across the field and into the woods, retracing a path that my own two feet had never before touched.

The next week, my last week of camp, Ricki felt well enough to return. Laughing made her chest hurt, and so did talking loud, so she couldn't do more than sit outside the ring and watch us perform for her final evaluation.

I packed carrots for Sparky and sugar cubes and every apple we had in our fruit bin. I didn't know how else to say good-bye. Instead of watching the other campers execute the set routine that Ricki had rehearsed with us, I brushed Sparky until her coat gleamed and Mitch called for the *R*s in the alphabet of camper names. And then Sparky and I executed the specified maneuvers because, really, they only required my two eyes and her four legs. She didn't fidget in place when I lifted each of her hooves, removed the halter and bridled her, mounted, dismounted, and then mounted again. She both walked and trotted in figure eights along the flagged poles, never brushing a single one. Sparky backed up, turned circles, left and right, cantered at the first signal, and stopped exactly along-side Ricki in the bleachers. I didn't have to ask her twice to do anything. And yet, instead of being pleased or proud, I felt only relief as I dismounted. How could I ride Sparky as though her blindness didn't matter?

On Friday, after the awards in boating and camp crafts and nature studies, Ricki presented her awards. The newer kids became Colts; some attained Yearling status; and some of the advanced riders, Thoroughbred. Moving very slowly, Ricki presented each of us a certificate and a card for a wallet, which, of course, none of us had. Maybe because I already had two

Thoroughbred cards from previous summers, Ricki left me out of the roll.

Then Ricki returned to her seat, gathered her backpack, and walked over, maybe to explain. But when she stood in front of me, instead of a whisper she announced, "This year, we have a special achievement honor, The Pegasus Award . . . " My heart beat so loudly I couldn't hear any of her words, let alone my name. As Ricki pressed a blue-ribboned card and a small trophy of a winged horse into my hands, I heard her say, "Just don't hug me. Congratulations!" I couldn't keep my eyes from filling with tears again, the happy kind, at least in part. The clapping grew loud, like the horse hooves echoing from the planks of our ravine bridge.

"Ricki," I forced myself to say her name. "Ricki, did you know that Sparky is blind?"

"Of course, yes."

"But—but *I* didn't. I cantered all those days in the field, and she could have fallen in the, in the holes, and Gibby—"

"Any horse can fall. But most always, they don't. You're a good rider, a careful one, and Sparky's eyesight is just about as important as her saddle color when it comes to riding. But . . . well . . . maybe I should have pointed that out."

The applause had stopped by now, and Mitch, crouching behind my knees, had pulled me onto his shoulders and stood.

"Bravo, Pegasus!" he exclaimed, while the other kids in my group leaped up to smack my butt as though I'd scored the final point in some important game.

Before we left the stables, I went to Sparky's stall. Under the dim overhead bulb, I waved my hands in front of one eye, then the other. Her ears flickered with attention. Her nostrils flared as they gathered a scent she clearly recognized. What did I expect to see? Each wide-open eye had any other horse's gaze.

And that was it. I never saw Sparky again. I never rode another horse. As for Ricki and Mitch, and even some of my friends from that day camp—they, too, remain within that one particular summer.

Curiously, it's Gibby I continue to see. Not in person, but when I obsess about the cruel things that seem so natural to us as people—cruelties to animals, including our own kind—it's Gibby, just a blurry image of him that reappears, shouting the word "stupid," and firing dirt clods.

One other thing does reappear every now and then. This image of myself, stunned and weeping in the middle of that meadow. And while that twelve-year-old boy and, no doubt, that mythic horse, are long gone, I now can see—rather than the sun, woods, or other riders—my own reflection in that cloudy, uncomprehending, sparkling eye of my horse. It's not so different from who I am today.

✦　✦　✦

◆ ◆ ◆

Notes from Michael J. Rosen

"That fall, something else—writing, in fact—took the place of riding (funny, how close the sound of the two words), although it might have been any number of other things, since the vacuum within me had to fill.

I began to keep a notebook of poems, reveries, impressions of moods and seasons. There were drawings, too, washes with a rapidograph—a very fancy and troublesome pen that I'd seen some of the older kids in the art room using. And because this was the Sixties, my recorded thoughts alluded to the monumental issues of the era: the ongoing war in Vietnam, hunger in Biafra, drug abuse. Not that I had anything to *say* about those oppressive issues, but I'd found some way to *listen* to what was being said about them, and that was by putting words on paper. There, I could study, in revision after revision, one lingering image, as if taken by a camera's flash, of an overwhelming, complicated, faster-than-I-could-process world.

Perhaps that summer, giving up not only riding but the realm of childhood that accompanied it, is where I might trace not my talent for writing, but my need for it. The very next summer, I began to work at that same camp, as a counselor-in-training for the youngest children, and I remained at the camp, eventually becoming the director for the eleven- and twelve-year-olds, until I was twenty-six.

For more than twenty years, summer camp provided my happiest times. Yet, somehow, I've allowed this story to make me sound friendless and broody. Where is my family, who have been the steadiest, most loving part of my life? I suppose that to tell a story is to create another kind of vacuum, removing so much of the real, taken-for-granted world in order to pull the reader into one that can be knowable, and I hope kindred, in a few thousand words."

✦　✦　✦

Learning to Swim

✦

KYOKO MORI

I was determined to swim at least twenty-five meters in the front crawl. As we did every summer, my mother, younger brother, and I were going to stay with my grandparents, who lived in a small farming village near Himeji, in Japan. From their house, it was a short walk through some rice paddies to the river where my mother had taught me how to swim when I was six. First, she showed me how to float with my face in the water, stretching my arms out in front of me and lying very still so my whole body was like a long plastic raft full of air. If you thought about it that way, my mother said, floating was as easy as just standing around or lying down to sleep. Once I got comfortable with floating, she taught me to kick my legs and paddle my arms so I could move forward, dog-paddling with my face out of the water.

Now I was too old to dog-paddle like a little kid. My mother had tried to teach me the front crawl the previous summer. I knew what I was supposed to do—flutter kick and push the water from front to back with my arms, while keeping my face in the water and turning sideways to breathe—but somehow there seemed to be too much I had to remember all at once. I forgot to turn my head and found myself dog-paddling again after only a few strokes. This summer, I thought, I would work harder and learn to swim as smoothly and gracefully as my mother. Then I would go back to school in September and surprise my classmates and my teachers. At our monthly swimming test, I would swim the whole length of our pool and prove myself one of the better swimmers in our class.

At our school, where we had monthly tests to determine how far each of us could swim without stopping, everyone could tell who the best and the worst swimmers were by looking at our white cloth swimming caps. For every five or ten meters we could swim, our mothers sewed a red or black line on the front of the cap. At the last test we had, in late May, I had made it all the way across the width of the pool in an awkward combination of dog paddle and front crawl, earning the three red lines on my cap for fifteen meters. That meant I was an average swimmer, not bad, not great. At the next test, in September, I would have to try the length of the pool, heading toward the deep end. If I made it all the way across, I would earn five red lines for twenty-five meters. There were several kids in our class who had done that, but only one of them had turned around after touching the wall and swum farther, heading back toward the shallow end. He stopped halfway across, where the water was up to our chests. If he had gone all the way back, he would have earned five black lines, meaning "fifty meters and more." That was the highest mark.

All the kids who could swim the length of the pool were boys. They were the same boys I competed with every winter during our weekly race from the cemetery on the hill to our schoolyard. They were always in the first pack of runners to come back—as I was. I could beat most of them in the last dash across the schoolyard because I was a good sprinter, but in the pool they easily swam past me and went farther. I was determined to change that. There was no reason that I should spend my summers dog-paddling in the shallow end of the pool while these boys glided toward the deep end, their legs cutting through the water like scissors.

My brother and I got out of school during the first week of July and were at my grandparents' house by

July 7—the festival of the stars. On that night if the sky was clear, the Weaver Lady and the Cowherd Boy would be allowed to cross the river of Heaven—the Milky Way—for their once-a-year meeting. The Weaver Lady and the Cowherd Boy were two stars who had been ordered to live on opposite shores of the river of Heaven as punishment for neglecting their work when they were together.

On the night of the seventh, it was customary to write wishes on pieces of colored paper and tie them to pieces of bamboo. On the night of their happy meeting, the Weaver Lady and the Cowherd Boy would be in a generous mood and grant the wishes. I wished, among other things, that I would be able to swim the length of the pool in September. Of course I knew, as my mother reminded me, that no wish would come true unless I worked hard.

Every afternoon my mother and I walked down to the river in our matching navy blue swimsuits. We swam near the bend of the river where the current slowed. The water came up to my chest, and I could see schools of minnows swimming past my knees and darting in and out among the rocks on the bottom. First I practiced the front crawl, and then a new stroke my mother was teaching me: the breaststroke.

"A good thing about this stroke," she said, "is that

you come up for air looking straight ahead, so you can see where you are going."

We both laughed. Practicing the front crawl in the river—where there were no black lines at the bottom—I had been weaving wildly from right and left, adding extra distance.

As we sat together on the riverbank, my mother drew diagrams in the sand, showing me what my arms and legs should be doing. Then we lay down on the warm sand so I could practice the motions.

"Pretend that you are a frog," she said. "Bend your knees and then kick back. Flick your ankles. Good."

We got into the water, where I tried to make the motions I had practiced on the sand, and my mother swam underwater next to me to see what I was doing. It was always harder to coordinate my legs and arms in the water, but slowly, all the details that seemed so confusing at first came together, so I didn't have to think about them separately. My mother was a good teacher. Patient and humorous, she talked me out of my frustrations even when I felt sure I would never get better. By mid-August, in both the front crawl and the breaststroke, I could swim easily downstream—all the way to the rock that marked the end of the swimming area. My mother thought that the distance had to be at least fifty meters. When I reached the rock, I would turn around and swim against the current. It was harder going that way. I had to stop several times and rest, panting a little. But swimming in a pool where the water was still, I was sure I could easily go on for twenty-five meters.

Our grandparents' house was crowded during the summer because all our uncles and aunts visited, bringing their children. My mother had three brothers and one sister. My brother and I thought of our aunt's husband and our uncles' wives as being our uncle and aunts as well—never making a big distinction between who was and wasn't related to us by blood. Our cousins, though, did not think of our father as their uncle. He had never visited in the country with us, and even when my mother and her brothers or sister got together in town, he was out with his own friends or else he would retire to another room, scarcely acknowledging their presence. My cousins never called him "Uncle Hiroshi," the way my brother and I called their mothers "Aunt Michiyo" or "Aunt Saeko." Even to my brother and me, our father seemed less like family than our uncles, aunts, cousins, and grandparents.

That summer, during the third week of August, two of my uncles, their wives, and my mother decided to take a trip to the Sea of Japan for the weekend, bringing my brother, our cousins, and me. All of us kids were excited about going to the seacoast. It was on the less populated side of our country, which faced China, Korea, Russia, and other faraway northern places.

I had never been to that sea, though the river we swam in ended there. When my mother warned me not to swim past the rock that marked off the swimming area—because the current got strong— she said, "We don't want you carried past Ikaba, all the way to the Sea of Japan." Ikaba, a village to the north, got its name, which meant "fifty waves," because the river was so turbulent and wavy there. I imagined the water tumbling down rocky mountains from Ikaba to the faraway sea.

Our three families took a bus to the seacoast, arriving shortly after dusk. We checked into an old-fashioned inn, where all of us kids were to sleep in one big room. My uncles and aunts—the two couples— had their own rooms, and my mother stayed alone, as she always did on these trips since my father never came along. If she felt lonely or odd, she never said anything—as always, she was cheerful and talkative. At supper, she said that she could hear the sea in the dark, but I thought she was imagining it. Lying down on my futon later I heard only my cousins—younger than I—laughing and screaming as they rolled around on the floor or threw pillows at one another instead of going to sleep the way we were supposed to.

The next morning after breakfast, we dressed in our swimsuits and walked to the beach, which was just down the road from the inn. On a narrow strip of white sand, a few families were clustered around bright red, blue, and pink beach towels. Some people were already in the water. Even a long way out, the water came only to their waists or chests. Big waves were hitting the rocks on a piece of land that jutted out to the sea to our left. Maybe my mother had heard the waves hitting that desolate, rocky shore the night before, I thought. They pounded and crashed, muffling all the other sounds on the beach.

While my uncles and aunts and their kids spread out their beach towels on the sand, my mother and I walked to the water's edge, leaving my brother behind with my cousins. I had never swum in the sea before, but I had seen pictures in my geography book of people floating on the Dead Sea. The writing underneath said that the salt in the water made it easier for people to float.

The sea was cold as my mother and I walked in — much colder than the pool or the river — but it was a hot sunny morning. I knew I would get used to it soon. We went in and splashed around for a while; then I started practicing my front crawl.

I couldn't tell if it really was easier to float. A big

wave came and hit my face sideways just as I was turning my head to breathe. I stood up coughing. The water didn't taste like the salt water that I gargled with when I had a cold. Instead, it had a strong bitter taste that stung my nostrils and my throat. My eyes burned.

"Try floating on your back," my mother suggested, flopping back and closing her eyes. "It's easy."

She was right. In the pool, I could float on my stomach, but never on my back. But in the sea, my legs and head didn't start sinking while my chest and stomach stayed afloat. All of me was floating; I could almost take a nap.

Once we got tired of floating, my mother and I started jumping the waves. Side by side holding hands, we treaded water, each paddling with one arm instead of two, waiting for the next big wave to come surging our way. If we stopped moving at just the right time, we could crest over the top and glide down to the other side, falling slowly down the gentle slope till another wave came and lifted us up. All around us, other grownups and kids were doing the same thing. There were so many waves coming and going. Sometimes we couldn't see people who were only a few feet away until a wave lifted us up and dropped us almost on top of them. Laughing, we would apologize before another wave swept us away.

I don't know how long we were riding the waves

before I noticed that my mother and I hadn't seen anyone for a long time. I thought of another thing, too. When we first started, my feet had brushed against the sand bottom almost every time we came down. In the lull between the waves, I'd be standing in the water only up to my chest. That hadn't happened for a while. My feet hadn't touched bottom for at least twenty waves now. I stretched my body as straight as I could, trying to touch bottom with my toes. Nothing. Just as I opened my mouth to point that out to my mother, a big wave came, my head went under, and my hand was swept loose from hers. When I came up again, I was turned around, facing the shore for the first time. I couldn't believe what I saw. The people on the beach looked so small that I couldn't tell our family from anyone else's.

Before I really understood what this meant, another wave rose, my head went under again, and I came up coughing and spitting. My mother, to my relief, was right beside me, treading water.

"Mom," I tried to warn her, but the look on her face told me that she already knew. Her eyes were wide open and there was a big frown between her eyebrows.

"Turn around and swim," she said. "It's not as far as you think."

"I can't," I gasped before a wave pounded me, filling my mouth with a burning, bitter taste.

My mother was beside me again, treading water. She couldn't reach out and hold my hand now, I realized suddenly, because even she needed both of her arms to stay afloat. The water was moving underneath, pulling us sideways. The beach looked farther and farther away. It was all I could do to keep my head from going under.

My mother started flinging her hand upward, trying to wave it from side to side. She was calling for help. That meant we were drowning.

Before the next wave hit us, I kicked my legs as hard as I could and lunged toward my mother, making up the short distance between us. The wave hit. We came up, both of us coughing and spitting, my arms clutched tightly around her neck.

"Listen," my mother said, in a choked-up voice. "You have to let go."

"But I'll drown," I wailed.

She stopped moving her arms for just a moment— long enough to put them around me and draw me closer. I could feel my shoulders, wet and slippery, pressed against her collarbone. "Let go," she said in a voice that sounded surprisingly calm. "Now, or we'll both drown."

By the time the next wave went over my head I was swimming alone, flailing my arms and legs to come up for air, and my mother was beside me. If it weren't for me, I thought, she could easily swim back to the shore. She was a strong swimmer. We were drowning because of me.

"Stay calm," she said, "and float."

We treaded water for a while, and between the waves my mother looked around, no doubt trying to measure the distance we had to swim.

"Look over there," she said, turning away from the shore and pointing toward the piece of land jutting into the sea. "We can't swim back to the beach, but we can make it to those rocks."

The waves had been pushing us sideways, toward the rocks, as well as farther from the shore. From where we were now, the tip of that land was about as far away as I could swim in the river without stopping if the current was with me. That piece of land was our last chance. If I couldn't make it there, I would surely drown: Heading toward the rocks meant turning away from the beach completely, swimming farther out to sea. If I drifted too far to the side and missed the tip of the land, there wouldn't be anywhere else. Every time I came up for air, I'd better be looking at those rocks, making sure they were still in my sight. The only stroke that would allow me to do that was the breaststroke.

I took a big breath and started kicking my legs with my knees bent, flicking my ankles the way my mother had taught me in the river. The arms, I told myself, should draw nice big arcs, not a bunch of little frantic circles that would make me tired. My mother swam right beside me in her easy graceful breaststroke — she was between me and the rest of the sea, guiding me toward the rocks, showing me how I should swim.

The waves we had been fighting were suddenly helping us. In just a few minutes, my mother and I stood on the rocky ground of that slip of land, looking back toward the shore. My legs felt wobbly, and I was breathing hard. The two of us looked at each other, too stunned to say anything. For a while we just stood trying to catch our breath, listening to the waves as they continued to crash at our feet. Then we started walking. The rocks formed a steep cliff above us, but at the bottom, there was enough room for us to walk side by side. Cautiously we picked our way back to the beach, trying not to cut our feet or slip back into the sea. On the way we noticed a group of people gathered on the sand, watching us. When we got there, they came rushing toward us. They were my uncles and several other men we had never seen.

"I waved for help," my mother said to them.

"We thought you were just waving for fun," one of my uncles said. "We didn't know anything was wrong until we saw you walking on those rocks."

One of the strangers, an old man in a shirt and trousers, shook his head. "You got caught in a rip tide," he said. "A fisherman drowned there a few years ago."

Several people were talking all at once, saying how lucky we were, but I wasn't listening very carefully. My brother was running toward us. Behind him, the beach was more crowded than when we had first started swimming. For the first time, I noticed an ice cream stand not too far away.

"Mom," I said. "My throat hurts from the seawater. I would love some ice cream."

When my mother told people the story of our near drowning, that was the detail she always emphasized—how I had calmly asked for ice cream as soon as we were back on the beach. Every time we remembered this incident, she said to me, "You are a brave girl. You let go of me when you had to."

The way she talked about it, our experience in the Sea of Japan was a great adventure that proved my courage: If I could swim well enough not to drown in a place where a fisherman had died in a rip tide, then I never again had to worry about drowning. I did not question her logic—though years later I realized that my mother had said just the right things to prevent me from becoming afraid. If she had told stories of a near disaster, a close call—instead of the story about my courage—I might never have been able to swim again. Instead I believed that I had conquered that sea for good. All I had to do was be more careful and watch out for the rip tide. My mother and I swam at the same beach again the same afternoon and the two following days; we returned to my grandparents' house and continued our swimming lessons. I was getting so good, she said, that the following year she would teach me the butterfly.

Back at school in September, I swam the length of the pool in the breaststroke without stopping. When I got to the end, I touched the edge of the pool and turned around. The other side of the pool didn't look nearly as far away as the shore had from the sea the day I had almost drowned. The water wasn't moving or trying to pull me under. It was nothing. I started swimming back, past the first five meters where the pool was deep, then past the ten-meter mark, past the halfway mark, where the only other student from my class had stopped. I took a deep breath, changed to the front crawl, and swam all the way to the end. My hand hit the wall; I stood up. My mother would be pleased, I thought, to sew five black lines on my cap.

. . .

Though I did not know it then, that winter, when my mother turned thirty-eight, she began to be overcome by her unhappiness—not about me or my brother, but about her life in general and especially about the way my father seldom came home to spend time with her. In the next three years, this unhappiness grew heavier every day—till it was something she could not bear alone. My father stayed away more once he sensed her unhappiness. My brother and I were too young to fully understand what was happening, though we both knew deep down that something was terribly wrong. My mother had been the oldest of five children, the one who always took care of her younger siblings and helped her parents. She could not imagine confiding in her family and burdening them.

When I was twelve, my mother decided to die rather than to live the rest of her life crippled by unhappiness, unable to stir from the chair where she spent her afternoons weeping. She left me a note in which she told me these things and more. "You are a strong and cheerful person by nature," she wrote to me. "The way I am, with my unhappiness, I am no good to you. I'm afraid I would only hurt you by being around. You must go on alone without me. At first you will be sad, I know, but you will overcome your sorrow. Be strong. Be happy for me."

Her choice is not one I would make now if I ever found myself drowning in unhappiness. I would try everything to live. But I understand my mother, too. She had told me to let go of her when we were both drowning in the sea. Though I wanted to cling to her then, I knew that I could not. When she decided to die, she must have remembered that time. She was asking me, again, to let her go—to let her float deeper out to the sea, where she could be at peace, while I swam with all my strength back to the rocks. She wanted me to live and to be brave. Swimming now in the clear-water lakes of Wisconsin, where I live, I sometimes imagine my mother riding the waves of the sea, cresting over the top and falling gently without ever hitting bottom, laughing her easy musical laugh. She could be right next to me: We are separated only by glimmering water.

✦ ✦ ✦

✦ ✦ ✦

Notes from Kyoko Mori

"I decided to write about my experience in the Sea of Japan because it was by far the most dramatic thing that happened in my childhood. I have changed a few details of geography, and the 'real' experience happened in another language, but otherwise, the details are close to the facts from my past. Even when the facts are 'true,' though, our minds shape our memories. No matter what we write about, the distinction between fact and fiction, memory and story, is as elusive as the constantly moving wall of water that separates one swimmer from another.

I have always wanted to become a writer. In those summers that my mother, brother, and I stayed at my grandparents' house, my grandfather and I used to sit side by side every morning, writing in our diaries. In first and second grades, I had a diary that was divided in half: The top half was for pictures, the bottom half for words. As I grew older, words replaced all the pictures — *became* the pictures, which was just as well. Although I loved to draw and paint, and I still love to look at art, even in third or fourth grade I knew that words came easier to me than lines and angles.

My mother and her family encouraged me to write. My grandfather had been a schoolteacher, though he was retired by the time I was born. My mother, like her father, kept a diary and wrote weekly letters home to her parents during the year, describing the flowers in her garden, the cookies she and I had baked, the new clothes she was making for us, some funny thing my brother had said. Two of my uncles—my mother's younger brothers—are teachers. Because I am the oldest of all the children in my extended family, I remember the things my brother and cousins were too young to remember: When I was young, our grandfather was still strong enough to go walking in the mountains with me; my grandmother grew more flowers and vegetables than she did years later when my cousins were in grade school. So in a way, I always thought it was my duty— as well as my pleasure—to write down the family stories: To record, describe, and re-create the past so that it will never be lost."

✦　✦　✦

Waiting for Midnight

◆

KAREN HESSE

In the early 1960s, I lived in a neighborhood in Baltimore city where everyone pretty much knew everyone else.

Our parents gathered on weekends for community barbecues while we kids, in shifting patterns, flocked from one friend's yard to another. In good weather, seven or eight of us would park our behinds on the corner stoop and put on a talent show. And every night, up and down our block, fathers would come out on their porches and call their children home.

"Harry!" That was Mr. Izzy.

"Bonnie!" That was Mr. Maish.

"Howard Brucey!" Howard Bruce's father had a voice so deep, he might have been calling Howard Bruce all the way from heaven.

My father didn't call me. I came home after my last friend vanished from the block.

Maybe my father's day job as a collection man exhausted him too much to come looking for me; maybe the constant battles between my parents kept them from noticing that it had grown dark and I hadn't yet come home. Whatever the reason, I didn't mind. I hated when evening came. I dreaded going to bed, because in my bedroom, at night, voices haunted me.

They whispered to me, whispered secrets, secrets I couldn't tell anyone.

Secrets about myself.

Secrets about my parents.

Secrets about the woman in the house next door. I was an unwilling conspirator in my next-door neighbor's secret. Her secret was so big, so cruel, it filled her own house and spilled over into mine. The secret of the woman next door was that every night, somewhere around midnight, she'd lock her children in an upstairs closet and wouldn't let them out again 'til morning.

Our row houses, on West Garrison Avenue, mirrored each other. The closet in the house next door was an exact reflection of my own. Those closets were small, too small for me to stay in for very long, much too small for the kids next door to spend each night in. All through the long hours, those children stood, jammed together inside that dark, airless closet, pleading with their mother to be let out. "Please," they would whisper. "Please, Mommy. We'll be good. Pleeease."

I heard every cry they uttered, every rise of panic, every whimper. Sleepless, I listened in my room, my bed pressed against the common wall between our two houses.

The secret of those children I kept along with all my other secrets. That's the way things were back then. You didn't interfere in anyone's private stuff, and no one interfered in yours.

I found ways to get through the night. I read under the covers using a flashlight; I made up stories inside my head, retelling those same stories at our neighborhood talent show the next day. I never told the truth about how things were for me or for the kids next door. Instead I kept my friends riveted to the stoop as I spun tales born out of my nightly need to escape the whispering.

Through most of my childhood my mother worked as a receptionist at Margo-Lynn Beauty Parlor. My father drove down the dusty back roads on the outskirts of Baltimore, collecting weekly payments from the poorest families, as they purchased, a dollar or two at a time, a new refrigerator or a new stove. When I got sick, neither of my parents could stay home from work. I went to school every day, regardless of how I felt. But on the days the school nurse sent me back home again, I stayed with Bubi Hannah.

Bubi Hannah lived with her daughter and son-in-law, in the row house two doors down from ours. Once, after coming home midway through the morning, I threw up all over Bubi Hannah's sofa. She never even got upset. She just cleaned it up, flipped the cushions over, and patting them smooth said, "Shirley'll never notice."

When I stayed at Bubi Hannah's house, sometimes I could hear the woman next door. She would pace, muttering to herself. I would look to Bubi Hannah, to see if she heard, too. Bubi Hannah would gaze into my face, her eyes moist. I wondered if Bubi Hannah knew about the children and the closet, too, but I couldn't bring myself to ask.

When I was ten, I read a story.

The story took place during Shavuos, a Jewish holiday that falls somewhere around the end of May. The hero of the story, K'Tonton, a Jewish Tom Thumb, plans to make a wish for himself at midnight on Shavuos, when he believes the sky will open and his wish will be granted. At the climax of the story, the sky does open, however K'Tonton doesn't spend the wish on himself. In the end, he uses it to help another.

It was a simple, moralistic tale, but arresting nonetheless, because it gave me hope that God might intervene if only I spoke out at just the right moment, in just the right way. I had plenty to speak out about: The way my parents were with each other, the way my mother was with herself, the way it was for the kids next door, the way it was for me.

I rarely saw the children next door, except occasionally when they twitched open their living-room curtains and peered out. They didn't attend public school. Their mother had made other arrangements. She had once taught school herself. My mother said she had been brilliant. But she had suffered a nervous breakdown and received no help, and that was supposed to explain everything.

We were told not to go trick-or-treating at her house, but never told why. We wouldn't have gone anyway. She scared all of us. Me, because I knew what she did to her children; the others, because she was so strange. Being near her felt like standing too close to a high-voltage wire.

It was impossible to avoid her, though. She would come out on her porch while I played jacks on mine.

"Hello, Karen," she'd say.

I'd feel myself stiffen as I said hello back.

"Have you read the newspaper today, Karen?" she'd ask.

I'd shake my head.

"How do you expect to learn?" She'd sound almost calm, but there was something in her voice that made my skin crawl.

"You'll never get anywhere if you aren't informed," she'd say. She'd stare at me, force me to look back at her.

I would slip off the porch as soon as I dared and race up the block, away from her, thinking all the while that her own children couldn't do what I had just done. They couldn't race up the block, they couldn't get away from her, not ever.

When I did catch a glimpse of her children—the girl, a few years older than I was, the boy, a year or two younger—the whiteness of their skin startled me. So pale, they were completely untouched by the Maryland sun, completely untouched by anyone or anything that wasn't in that house. No one knew them. I knew only their voices, only their desperation.

Meanwhile in my own house my mother sickened; dark circles under her eyes, no appetite, so thin a slight wind might blow her over. Her illness seemed connected to her unhappiness with my father, though I didn't understand how. Twice my mother went to the hospital. Each time she nearly died. Her doctor instructed me to take care of her: Do nothing to upset her; say nothing to upset her.

Each morning before I left for school, and each afternoon when I returned home, I would scramble eggs for my mother. I learned to make them moist, the way she liked them. From the time I left until the time I returned, and all through the evening and the long nights, my mother ate only those eggs. As I stood over the frying pan twice a day, I'd try to think good things, healing things, hoping those thoughts would enter the eggs and make my mother better.

"When is Shavuos?" I asked my father one evening.

On Shabbos and the holidays, my father served as cantor at a Reform synagogue in Baltimore. He sat on the bimah with the rabbi and led the congregation in song. I was approaching the age of thirteen, when Jewish children are admitted as adult members to the religious community, but my parents never mentioned my studying Torah or having a bas mitzvah.

"Shavuos?" my father said. "It's next week. Why? You want to come to services?"

"No," I said.

I couldn't go to services. I had to be home and awake when the sky opened at midnight, to wish for my mother and father, to wish for the children next door, to wish for myself.

The night of Shavuos I sat in the living room alone, watching television. My father left for services early; my mother had already shut herself in her bedroom for the night.

I climbed the stairs to my room around ten, washed, and changed into my pajamas. I listened for sounds from next door. The closet was quiet.

Closing my bedroom door, I turned out the light and stood at the dressing table in front of my window. *Less than two hours 'til midnight,* I thought, gazing into the sky. Surely I could stay awake for two hours.

My father came home a little after eleven.

As soon as their bedroom door shut, my parents started fighting. The air in the house prickled with their anger. The fight was a short one though. Within a few minutes the house grew quiet again; I heard only the occasional pop of a floorboard and the drip of the kitchen sink.

I thought everyone in the world had gone to sleep. It was just me and God now, on either side of the sky, waiting for midnight.

Still quiet next door. Maybe tonight, maybe just for tonight, it would stay quiet. I looked over my shoulder at my closet. My mother used to hang a calendar on the door and put gold stars on it for the days I didn't cry. I rarely earned more than a handful of gold stars in any particular year. She eventually gave up on the gold stars. I eventually stopped crying.

On that night of Shavuos, my feet grew cold as I stood waiting. My legs ached. I decided to climb into bed.

But I feared falling asleep and missing my appointment with heaven. To stay awake, I put my day clothes back on. I pulled my shirt back over my head, slipped into my pants, and sat upright in bed, leaning my cheek against the cool white wall. The time crept slowly forward. Once, I nodded off and started back awake. Rubbing my eyelids with the knuckles of my thumbs, I made myself stand and walk to the dressing table under the window.

I didn't need a flashlight. I could read my watch by the moon. The time was 11:39.

I wanted it to happen. I wanted the sky to open. I wanted to see inside heaven.

As I stared up into the night, a dog came down the alley and turned over a garbage can across the way. I shifted my eyes from the sky for a moment, down to the dog pawing trash, then quickly back up again. I didn't dare risk looking away any longer.

At five minutes to midnight, I tucked my chair in under my dressing table and leaned toward the window.

That's when, next door, the voices started.

"Please," the girl whispered. "Please. Let us out. We'll be good. I promise. We'll be good. Please let us out, Mommy. Pleeeease."

She sounded like a ghost, her voice coming softly through the closet wall. I turned toward the sound.

And that's when it happened. I sensed the change.

Quickly turning back toward the window, I saw it.

The filmy black of the night split open, and streaming out through the opening were the most exquisite colors. They swirled around and around, a dazzling display of radiance.

Out of that shimmering brightness, ladders unfurled. I could not see them clearly, and yet I knew they were ladders. And down those ladders, beings descended. Brilliant beings of light. They were angels. I was seeing angels.

I don't think I breathed. I don't think I blinked. My eyes wide, I took in every detail.

And then, just like that, the ladders disappeared, the colors vanished, and the night returned to its filmy blackness.

The entire scene had taken place in a heartbeat.

And I had not made any wish at all.

I had not wished for my parents to stop fighting, I had not wished for my mother to be well, I had not wished for the end of the children's suffering next door, I had not wished for the end of my own torment. I had stood before the face of God and wished for nothing.

K'Tonton, at least, had made a wish.

I wanted to cry, and yet my eyes stayed dry and round with wonder. I stood watching the black sky for a long time.

Next door, the pleading of the children grew quieter and quieter.

And finally, during a stretch of silence, I curled up on my bed and dozed off.

Suddenly I awoke. A different kind of light ricocheted off my bedroom walls. The light from heaven had filled me with awe, but this light filled me with terror. It paced around and around my room, like a caged animal.

Still dressed, I crept to my window, my heart thrumming in my neck. I saw two police cars in the alley below, lights rotating on their roofs, the low squawk of their radios crackling into the night. And then I saw the shadowy figure of a child, wrapped in a blanket, being brought out of the house next door and placed into one of the cruisers. A second child already sat huddled in the same cruiser's back seat. Alone, in a cruiser in front of theirs, rigid, unflinching, sat their mother.

Bubi Hannah stood inside her gate, her arms wrapped around herself. She wore a coat over her nightgown. Her hair, in a long white braid, hung down her back.

The police cars pulled away at last, and as their lights vanished, I realized my closet was silent. Completely silent.

I felt almost weightless.

The rest of that night I slept sweetly, peacefully, for the first time in I couldn't remember how long. I slept deeper than the voice of Howard Bruce's father, a sleep that might have come all the way from Heaven.

✦ ✦ ✦

Notes from Karen Hesse

"This was a hard story to share. But I chose to relate this moment in my life because it marked a turning point for me. On that night, the night that I've transformed into the climax for this story, a flame of faith was kindled in my soul. During that night, for the first time, I saw that no matter how desperate and unrelenting things seemed, in a moment the situation could change and there could be respite, comfort, hope. I have modified the story a bit; left pieces out, put pieces in; but the core of this story is true.

I learned at a very early age the reward of retreating into fictional worlds. Not only did reading give me an escape from a difficult childhood, but the characters shared their survival skills with me, skills that I could then mold, shape, and apply to my own life.

My roots as a writer extend all the way back to those long Baltimore nights. I never imagined that the stories I told myself in that little room on West Garrison Avenue would blossom into a life's work. I simply wove those tales to console myself.

I am still awed by the things people survive, how people can turn their most crippling trials into soaring triumphs. Telling their stories is what compels me to write."

✦   ✦   ✦

* * *

The Snapping Turtle

✦

JOSEPH BRUCHAC

My grandmother was working in the flower garden near the road that morning when I came out with my fishing pole. She was separating out the roots of iris. As far as flowers go, she and I were agreed that iris had the sweetest scent. Iris would grow about anywhere, shooting up green sword-shaped leaves like the mythical soldiers that sprang from the planted teeth of a dragon. But iris needed some amount of care. Their roots would multiply so thick and fast that they could crowd themselves right up out of the soil. Spring separating and replanting were, as my grandmother put it, just the ticket.

Later that day, I knew, she would climb into our blue 1951 Plymouth to drive around the back roads of Greenfield, a box of iris in the back seat. She would stop at farms where she had noticed a certain color of iris that she didn't have yet. Up to the door she would go to ask for a root so that she could add another splash of color to our garden. And, in exchange, she would give that person, most often a flowered-aproned and somewhat elderly woman like herself, some of her own iris.

It wasn't just that she wanted more flowers herself. She had a philosophy. If only one person keeps a plant, something might happen to it. Early frost, insects, animals, Lord knows what. But if many have that kind of plant, then it may survive. Sharing meant a kind of immortality. I didn't quite understand it then, but I enjoyed taking those rides with her, carrying boxes and cans and flowerpots with new kinds of iris back to the car.

"Going fishing, Sonny?" she said now.

Of course, she knew where I was going. Not only the evidence of the pole in my hand, but also the simple facts that it was a Saturday morning in late May and I was a boy of ten, would have led her to that natural conclusion. But she had to ask. It was part of our routine.

"Un-hun," I answered, as I always did. "Unless you and Grampa need some help." Then I held my breath, for though my offer of aid had been sincere enough, I really wanted to go fishing.

Grama thrust her foot down on the spading fork, carefully levering out a heavy clump of iris marked last fall with a purple ribbon to indicate the color. She did such things with half my effort and twice the skill, despite the fact I was growing, as she put it, like a weed. "No, you go on along. This afternoon Grampa and I could use some help, though."

"I'll be back by then," I said, but I didn't turn and walk away. I waited for the next thing I knew she would say.

"You stay off of the state road, now."

In my grandmother's mind, Route 9N, which came down the hill past my grandparents' little gas station and general store on the corner, was nothing less than a Road of Death. If I ever set foot on it, I would surely be as doomed as our four cats and two dogs that met their fates there.

"Runned over and kilt," as Grampa Jesse put it.

Grampa Jesse, who had been the hired man for my grandmother's parents before he and Grama eloped, was not a person with book learning like my college-educated grandmother. His family was Abenaki Indian, poor but honest hill people who could read the signs in the forest, but who had never traipsed far along the trails of schoolhouse ways. Between Grama's books and Grampa's practical knowledge, some of which I was about to apply to bring home a mess of trout, I figured I was getting about the best education a ten-year-old boy could have. I was lucky that my grandparents were raising me.

"I'll stay off the state road," I promised. "I'll just follow Bell Brook."

Truth be told, the state road made me a little nervous, too. It was all too easy to imagine myself in the place of one of my defunct pets, stunned by the elephant bellow of a tractor-trailer's horn, looking wild-eyed up to the shiny metal grill; the thud, the lightning-bolt flash of light, and then the eternal dark. I imagined my grandfather shoveling the dirt over me in a backyard grave next to that of Lady, the collie, and Kitty-kitty, the gray cat, while my grandmother dried her eyes with her apron and said, "I told him to stay off that road!"

I was big on knowledge but very short on courage in those years. I mostly played by myself because the other kids my age from the houses and farms scattered around our rural township regarded me as a Grama's boy who would tell if they were to tie me up and threaten to burn my toes with matches, a ritual required to join the local society of pre-teenage boys. A squealer. And they were right.

I didn't much miss the company of other kids. I had discovered that most of them had little interest in the living things around them. They were noisier than Grampa and I were, scaring away the rabbits that we could creep right up on. Instead of watching the frogs catching flies with their long, gummy tongues, those boys wanted to shoot them with their BB guns. I couldn't imagine any of them having the patience or inclination to hold out a hand filled with sunflower seeds, as Grampa had showed me I could, long enough for a chickadee to come and light on an index finger.

Even fishing was done differently when I did it Grampa's way. I knew for a fact that most of those boys would go out and come home with an empty creel. They hadn't been watching for fish from the banks as I had in the weeks before the trout season began, so they didn't know where the fish lived. They didn't know how to keep low, float your line in, wait for that first tap, and then, after the strike that bent your pole, set the hook. And they never said thank-you to every fish they caught, the way I remembered to do.

Walking the creek edge, I set off downstream. By mid-morning, my bait can of moss and red earthworms that Grampa and I had dug from the edge of our manure pile was near empty. I'd gone half a mile and had already caught seven trout. All of them were squaretails, native brook trout whose sides were patterned with a speckled rainbow of bright circles— red, green, gold. I'd only kept the ones more than seven inches long, and I'd remembered to wet my hand before taking the little ones off the hook. Grasping a trout with a dry hand would abrade the slick coat of natural oil from the skin and leave it open for infection and disease.

As always, I'd had to keep the eyes in the back of my head open just as Grampa had told me to do whenever I was in the woods.

"Things is always hunting one another," he'd said.

And he was right. Twice, at places where Bell Brook swung near Mill Road I'd had to leave the stream banks to take shelter when I heard the ominous crunch of bicycle tires on the gravel. Back then, when I was ten, I was smaller than the other boys my age. I made up for it by being harder to catch. Equal parts of craftiness and plain old panic at being collared by bullies I viewed as close kin to Attila the Hun kept me slipperier than an eel.

From grapevine tangles up the bank, I'd watched as Pauly Roffmeier, Ricky Holstead, and Will Backus rolled up to the creek, making more noise than a herd of hippos, to plunk their own lines in. Both times, they caught nothing. It wasn't surprising, since they were talking like jaybirds, scaring away whatever fish might have been within half a mile. And Will kept lighting matches and throwing them down to watch them hiss out when they struck the water. Not to mention the fact that I had pulled a ten-inch brook trout out of the first hole and an eleven incher out of the second before they even reached the stream.

I looked up at the sky. I didn't wear a watch then. No watch made by man seemed able to work more than a few days when strapped to my wrist. It was a common thing on my Grampa's side of the family. "We jest got too much 'lectricity in us," he explained.

Without a watch, I could measure time by the sun. I could see it was about ten. I had reached the place where Bell Brook crossed under the state road. Usually I went no further than this. It had been my boundary for years. But somewhere along the way I had decided that today would be different. I think perhaps a part of me was ashamed of hiding from the other boys, ashamed of always being afraid. I wanted to do something that I'd always been afraid to do. I wanted to be brave.

I had no need to fish further. I had plenty of trout for our supper. I'd cleaned them all out with my Swiss Army knife, leaving the entrails where the crows and jays could get them. If you did that, the crows and jays would know you for a friend and not sound the alarm when they saw you walking in the woods. I sank the creel under water, wedged it beneath a stone. The water of the brook was deep and cold and I knew it would keep the flesh of the trout fresh and firm. Then

I cached my pole and bait can under the spice bushes. As I looked up at the highway, Grama's words came back to me:

"Stay off the state road, Sonny."

"*Under*," I said aloud, "is not *on*."

Then, taking a deep breath, bent over at the waist, I waded into the culvert that dove under the Road of Death. I had gone no more than half a dozen steps before I walked into a spider web so strong that it actually bounced me back. I splashed a little water from the creek up onto it and watched the beads shape a pattern of concentric circles. The orb-weaver sat unmoving in a corner, one leg resting on a strand of the web. She'd been waiting for the vibration of some flying creature caught in the sticky strands of her net. Clearly, I was much more than she had hoped for. She sat there without moving. Her wide back was patterned with a shape like that of a red and gold hourglass. Her compound eyes, jet black on her head, took in my giant shape. Spiders gave some people the willies. I knew their bite would hurt like blue blazes, but I still thought them graced with great beauty.

"Excuse me," I said. "Didn't mean to bother you."

The spider raised one front leg. A nervous reaction, most likely, but I raised one hand back. Then I ducked carefully beneath the web, entering an area where the light was different. It was like passing from one world into another. I sloshed through the dark culvert, my fingertips brushing the rushing surface of the stream, the current pushing at my calves. My sneakered feet barely held their purchase on the ridged metal, slick with moss.

When I came out the other side, the sunlight was blinding. Just ahead of me the creek was overarched with willows. They were so thick and low that there was no way I could pass without either going underwater or breaking a way through the brush. I wasn't ready to do either. So I made my way up the bank, thinking to circle back and pick up the creek farther down. For what purpose, I wasn't sure, aside from just wanting to do it. I was nervous as a hen yard when a chicken hawk is circling overhead. But I was excited, too. This was new ground to me, almost a mile from home. I'd gone farther from home in the familiar directions of north and west, into the safety of the woods, but this was different: Across the state road, in the direction of town; someone else's hunting territory. I stayed low to the ground and hugged the edges of the brush as I moved. Then I saw something that drew me away from the creek: The glint of a wider expanse of water. The Rez, the old Greenfield Reservoir.

I'd never been to the Rez, though I knew the other

boys went there. As I'd sat alone on the bus, my book-bag clasped tightly to my chest, I'd heard them talk about swimming there, fishing for bass, spearing bullfrogs five times as big as the little frogs in Bell Brook.

I knew I shouldn't be there, yet I was. Slowly I moved to the side of the wide trail that led to the edge of the deep water, and it was just as well that I did: Their bikes had been stashed in the brush down the other side of the path. They'd been more quiet than usual. I might have walked up on them if I hadn't heard a voice.

"Gimme a drag," a voice said, just over the edge of the bank. I slid back, my heart pounding so hard I knew that it sounded like a drum solo.

"You let it go out, jerk," answered another voice that I could barely hear over my deafening heartbeat.

"I'll light it."

I'll light it. Not, There he is. Let's kill him? I hadn't been heard or seen! I was still safe. But I was as curious as I was afraid. What were they doing? I had to see.

I picked up some of the dark mud with my fingertips and drew lines across my cheeks. Grampa had explained it would make me harder to see. Then I slid to a place where an old tree leaned over the bank, cloaked by the cattails that grew from the edge of the Rez. I made my way out on the trunk and looked. What I saw shocked me. Pauly and Ricky and Will were worse boys than I'd thought. They were really bad! They had a cigarette and they were smoking it.

"Gimme," Ricky said again. "I'm the one who brought it."

"Stole it from your Mommy's handbag, you mean." Pauly held Ricky at arm's length as he puffed and then coughed. "An whyn't you get more than one?"

"If I stole a fresh pack, she would've known for sure. Gimme! I'm the one's gonna be in Dutch if she finds out."

No, I thought. *You're wrong. All of you are going to get in trouble after I tell Grama what I've seen and she gets through calling all your parents.*

As I watched, they shared the cigarette, alternately puffing at it, coughing, dropping it, and relighting it. Finally, when Ricky had puffed down to the filter, the last to get it, their smoking orgy was over. Ricky flicked the butt into the Rez and stared out at the water. "It's not gonna come up," Ricky said. He picked up something that looked like a makeshift spear. "You lied."

"I did not. It was over there. The biggest snapper I ever saw." Will shaded his eyes with one hand and looked right in my direction without seeing me. "If we catch it, we could sell it for ten dollars to that colored man on Congress Street. They say snapping turtles have seven different kinds of meat in them."

"Crap," Pauly said, throwing his own spear aside.

"Let's go find something else to do."

One by one, they picked up their fishing poles and went back down the path. I waited without moving, hearing their heavy feet on the trail and then the rattle of their bike chains. I was no longer thinking about going home to tell Grama about their smoking. All I could think of was that snapping turtle.

I knew a lot about turtles. There were mud turtles and map turtles. There was the smart orange-legged wood turtle and the red-eared slider with its cheeks painted crimson as if it was going to war. Every spring Grama and Grampa and I would drive around, picking up those whose old migration routes had been cut by the recent and lethal ribbons of road. Spooked by a car, a turtle falls into that old defense of pulling head and legs and tail into its once impregnable fortress. But a shell does little good against the wheels of a Nash or a DeSoto.

Some days we'd rescue as many as a dozen turtles, taking them home for a few days before releasing them back into the wild. Painted turtles, several as big as two hands held together, might nip at you some, but they weren't really dangerous. And the wood turtles would learn in a day or so to reach out for a straw-berry or a piece of juicy tomato and then leave their heads out for a scratch while you stroked them with a finger.

Snappers though, they were different. Long-tailed, heavy-bodied and short-tempered, their jaws would gape wide and they'd hiss when you came up on them ashore. Their heads and legs were too big to pull into their shells and they would heave up on their legs and lunge forward as they snapped at you. They might weigh as much as fifty pounds, and it was said they could take off a handful of fingers in one bite. There wasn't much to recommend a snapping turtle as a friend.

Most people seemed to hate snappers. Snappers ate the fish and the ducks; they scared swimmers away. Or I should say that people hated them alive. Dead, they were supposed to be the best-eating turtle of all. *Ten dollars,* I thought. *Enough for me to send away to the mail-order pet place and get a pair of real flying squirrels.* I'd kept that clipping from *Field and Stream* magazine thumbtacked over my bed for four months now. A sort of plan was coming into my mind.

People were afraid of getting bit by snappers when they were swimming. But from what I'd read, and from what Grampa told me, they really didn't have much to worry about.

"Snapper won't bother you none in the water," Grampa said. If you were even to step on a snapping turtle resting on the bottom of a pond, all it would do would be to move away. On land, all the danger from a snapper was to the front or the side. From behind, a snapper couldn't get you. Get it by the tail, you were safe. That was the way.

And as I thought, I kept watch. And as I kept watch, I kept up a silent chant inside my mind.

Come here, I'm waiting for you.

Come here, I'm waiting for you.

Before long, a smallish log that had been sticking up farther out in the pond began to drift my way. It was, as I had expected, no log at all. It was a turtle's head. I stayed still. The sun's heat beat on my back, but I lay there like a basking lizard. Closer and closer the turtle came, heading right into water less than waist deep. It was going right for shore, for the sandy bank bathed in sun. I didn't think about why then, just wondered at the way my wanting seemed to have called it to me.

When it was almost to shore, I slid into the water on the other side of the log I'd been waiting on. The turtle surely sensed me, for it started to swing around as I moved slowly toward it, swimming as much as walking. But I lunged and grabbed it by the tail. Its tail was rough and ridged, as easy to hold as if coated with sandpaper. I pulled hard and the turtle came toward me. I stepped back, trying not to fall and pull it on top of me. My feet found the bank, and I leaned hard to drag the turtle out, its clawed feet digging into the dirt as it tried to get away. A roaring hiss like the rush of air from a punctured tire came out of its mouth, and I stumbled, almost losing my grasp. Then I took another step, heaved again, and it was mine.

Or at least it was until I let go. I knew I could not let go. I looked around, holding its tail, moving my feet to keep it from walking its front legs around to where it would snap at me. It felt as if it weighed a thousand pounds. I could only lift up the back half of its body. I started dragging it toward the creek, fifty yards away. It seemed to take hours, a kind of dance between me and the great turtle, but I did it. I pulled it back through the roaring culvert, water gushing over its shell, under the spider web, and past my hidden pole and creel. I could come back later for the fish. Now there was only room in the world for Bell Brook, the turtle, and me.

The long passage upstream is a blur in my memory. I thought of salmon leaping over falls and learned a little that day how hard such a journey must be. When I rounded the last bend and reached the place where the brook edged our property, I breathed a great sigh. But I could not rest. There was still a field and the back yard to cross.

My grandparents saw me coming. From the height of the sun it was now mid-afternoon, and I knew I was dreadful late.

"Sonny, where have you . . . ?" began Grama.

Then she saw the turtle.

"I'm sorry. It took so long because of . . ." I didn't finish the sentence because the snapping turtle, undaunted by his backward passage, took that opportunity to try once more to swing around and get me. I had to make three quick steps in a circle, heaving at its tail as I did so.

"Nice size turtle," Grampa Jesse said.

My grandmother looked at me. I realized then I must have been a sight. Wet, muddy, face and hands scratched from the brush that overhung the creek.

"I caught it at the reservoir," I said. I didn't think to lie to them about where I'd been. I waited for my grandmother to scold me. But she didn't.

"Jesse," she said, "Get the big washtub."

My grandfather did as she said. He brought it back and then stepped next to me.

"Leave go," he said.

My hands had a life of their own, grimly determined never to let loose of that all-too-familiar tail, but I forced them to open. The turtle flopped down. Before it could move, my grandfather dropped the big washtub over it. All was silent for a minute as I stood there, my arms aching as they hung by my side. Then the washtub began to move. My grandmother sat down on it and it stopped.

She looked at me. So did Grampa. It was wonderful how they could focus their attention on me in a way that made me feel they were ready to do whatever they could to help.

"What now?" Grama said.

"I heard that somebody down on Congress Street would pay ten dollars for a snapping turtle."

"Jack's," Grampa said.

My grandmother nodded. "Well," she said, "if you go now you can be back in time for supper. I thought we were having trout." She raised an eyebrow at me.

"I left them this side of the culvert by 9N," I said. "Along with my pole."

"You clean up and put on dry clothes. Your grandfather will get the fish."

"But I hid them."

My grandmother smiled. "Your grandfather will find them." And he did.

An hour later, we were on the way to Congress Street, the heart of the colored section of Saratoga Springs. In the 1950s, Congress Street was like a piece of Harlem dropped into an upstate town. We pulled up in front of Jack's, and a man who looked to be my grandfather's age got up and walked over to us. His skin was only a little darker than my grandfather's, and the two nodded to each other.

My grandfather put his hand on the trunk of the Plymouth.

"What you got there?" Jack said.

"Show him, Sonny."

I opened the trunk. My snapping turtle lifted up its head as I did so.

"I heard you might want to buy a turtle like this for ten dollars," I said.

Jack shook his head. "Ten dollars for a little one like that? I'd give you two dollars."

I looked at my turtle. Had it shrunk since Grampa wrestled it into the trunk?

"That's not enough," I said.

"Three dollars. My last offer."

I looked at Grampa. He shrugged his shoulders.

"I guess I don't want to sell it," I said.

"All right," Jack said. "You change your mind, come on back." He touched his hat with two fingers and walked back over to his chair in the sun.

As we drove back toward home, neither of us said anything for a while. Then my grandfather spoke.

"Would five dollars've been enough?"

"No," I said.

"How about ten?"

I thought about that. "I guess not."

"Why you suppose that turtle was heading for that sandbank?" Grampa said.

I thought about that, too. Then I realized the truth of it.

"It was coming out to lay its eggs."

"Might be."

I thought hard then. I'd learned it was never right for a hunter to shoot a mother animal, because it hurt the next generation to come. Was a turtle any different?

"Can we take her back?" I asked.

"Up to you, Sonny."

And so we did. Gramp drove the Plymouth right up the trail to the edge of the Rez. He held a stick so the turtle would grab onto it as I hauled her out of the trunk. I put her down and she just stayed there, her nose a foot from the water but not moving.

"We'll leave her," Grampa said. We turned to get into the car. When I looked back over my shoulder, she was gone. Only ripples on the water, widening circles rolling on toward other shores like generations following each other, like my grandmother's flowers still growing in a hundred gardens in Greenfield, like the turtles still seeking out that sandbank, like this story that is no longer just my own but belongs now to your memory, too.

✦ ✦ ✦

Notes from Joseph Bruchac

"When I think back on my childhood and the old house that I lived in with my grandparents, two images always come to mind. The first is books. Shelves and bookcases in every room filled with everything from leather-bound sets of Kipling and Dickens, Sir Walter Scott and Mark Twain and the Romantic poets to *Reader's Digest* condensed volumes which arrived in the mail every month. The books were my grandmother's, but as soon as I could read—and I was reading everything I could get my hands on by the time I was in second grade—I thought of them as mine, too. Grama was glad to share them with me, first by reading them aloud and then later by knowing just the right book to pull down from a high shelf and put into my hands.

The second image is of the little piece of forest behind our house—'The Woods' as my grandfather called it. Although Grampa Jesse could barely read a newspaper, he knew how to read the woods better than anyone I ever knew. The trees, the birds, the trails the animals made, he saw them all and shared them with me. Sometimes he did it without saying anything, just directing my attention the right way at just the right time—so I would see the robin's nest deep inside the spruce tree, its eggs as blue as a clear sky, so that I would realize those twigs and stones at the bottom of the stream were really the movable camouflaged homes of caddis fly larvae. He taught me to be careful about how I walked, about never taking too much of anything—whether it was the May flowers we picked to make bouquets or the trout from Bell Brook—and always to give something back. It might just be a word of thanks, but even a small gift meant something. It kept the balance.

My grandmother loved the outdoors, too, but her love was for the gardens she kept, the gardens I mention in this story. She always kept those gardens overflowing with flowers close to the roadside where everyone could see them and enjoy their beauty, so carefully planted that they were patterned like a patchwork quilt.

I think it was those two worlds—the world of books and the natural world that surrounded me as a child—that made me a writer. I wanted to share the things I saw and heard, the things I imagined. My grandparents were always sharing, and it just seemed like the natural thing to do. And whenever I wrote a poem or a story, both Grama and Grampa were eager to hear it and quick to tell me they had never heard anything quite like it before. So I kept on sharing and always trying to give something back.

That is why I chose to tell this story, a story that shows a little of those roots my grandparents nurtured."

✦ ✦ ✦

AUTHOR BIOGRAPHIES

NORMA FOX MAZER is the author of many highly acclaimed novels for young adults, including *After the Rain*, a Newbery Honor Book; *Taking Terri Mueller*, winner of the Edgar Allan Poe Award for Best Juvenile Novel; *A Figure of Speech*, a National Book Award nominee; and *Dear Bill, Remember Me? and Other Stories*, a *New York Times* Outstanding Book of the Year. Many of her novels have also been named Best Books for Young Adults by the American Library Association. She and her husband, the writer Harry Mazer, live in Jamesville, New York.

RITA WILLIAMS-GARCIA was raised in Seaside, California, and Jamaica, New York, where she currently lives. Her first novel, *Fast Talk on a Slow Track*, was named an American Library Association Best Book for Young Adults and an American Library Association Quick Pick for Reluctant Young Readers, and won the PEN/Norma Klein Award and a Parents' Choice Honor Award. Her second novel, *Like Sisters on the Homefront*, is a Coretta Scott King Honor Book.

PAUL FLEISCHMAN is the award-winning author of many books for children and young adults, including *Joyful Noise: Poems for Two Voices*, winner of the Newbery Medal; *Graven Images*, a Newbery Honor Book and a *Boston Globe—Horn Book* Honor Book; *Bull Run*, winner of the Scott O'Dell Award for Historical Fiction; *Saturnalia*, a *Boston Globe—Horn Book* Honor Book and an American Library Association Notable Children's Book; and *Dateline: Troy*, an American Library

Association Best Book for Young Adults. He lives in Pacific Grove, California.

JANE YOLEN has written and edited more than two hundred books and anthologies—for all age levels and in genres ranging from picture books to fantasy to science fiction. Her numerous awards include the Christopher Medal for *The Seeing Stick*; the National Jewish Book Award for *The Devil's Arithmetic*; the World Fantasy Award for *Favorite Folk Tales from Around the World*; and three honors for her body of work in children's literature: the Kerlan Award, the Keene State College Children's Literature Festival Award, and the Regina Medal. She and her husband divide their time between western Massachusetts and Scotland.

HOWARD NORMAN has translated and edited two collections of stories for young readers: *Trickster and the Fainting Bird,* and *The Girl Who Dreamed Only Geese and Other Tales of the Far North,* which won a Parents' Choice Honor Award and the Anne Izard Storytellers' Choice Award, and was nominated for the Dorothy Canfield Fisher Award. In addition, it was named a *New York Times Book Review* Best Illustrated Children's Book of the Year. Two of Howard Norman's novels for adults, *The Northern Lights* and *The Bird Artist*, have been chosen as National Book Award finalists. He and his wife, the poet Jane Shore, and their daughter Emma divide their time between Washington, D.C. and Vermont.

E. L. KONIGSBURG, the author of novels, short stories, and picture books, won her first Newbery Medal for the second novel she ever wrote, *From the Mixed-Up Files of Mrs. Basil E. Frankweiler*. That same year her first novel, *Jennifer, Hecate, Macbeth, William McKinley, and Me, Elizabeth*, was named a Newbery Honor Book. With *The View from Saturday*, published almost thirty years and more than fifteen books later, she won her second Newbery Medal. Born in New York City, E. L. Konigsburg lives in Florida.

MICHAEL J. ROSEN has written, edited, or illustrated more than thirty books for children and adults, including *Elijah's Angel*, winner of the National Jewish Book Award; *Speak! Children's Book Illustrators Brag About Their Favorite Dogs*; *The Heart Is Big Enough: Five Stories*; and *The Dog Who Walked with God*. Additionally, he has worked as literary director at The Thurber House, the writers' center in the restored home of James Thurber. Born and raised in Columbus, Ohio, he now lives in a forested area of central Ohio.

KYOKO MORI was born in Kobe, Japan. She moved to the United States at the age of twenty, originally to finish her undergraduate college degree. Her books for young adults include *One Bird* and *Shizuko's Daughter*, which was named an American Library Association Best Book for Young Adults, a *New York Times* Notable Book, and a *Publishers Weekly* Editors' Choice. Her most recent book for adults is *Polite Lies: On Being a Woman Caught Between Cultures*. Kyoko Mori currently lives in De Pere, Wisconsin, where she teaches creative writing at St. Norbert College.

KAREN HESSE grew up in Baltimore, Maryland, and now lives with her family in Vermont. She is the author of the Newbery Medal–winning *Out of the Dust*, which was also named a Best Book by *School Library Journal*, *Publishers Weekly*, and *Booklist*. Her other books for young readers include *Phoenix Rising*; *Letters from Rifka*; *The Music of Dolphins*, named an American Library Association Best Book for Young Adults and a Best Book by *Publishers Weekly* and *School Library Journal*; and *A Time of Angels*, named an International Reading Association Young Adults' Choice winner.

JOSEPH BRUCHAC is an author, storyteller, and editor who has drawn on his Native American heritage throughout his writing career. He has edited more than thirty books and has written more than sixty books of his own, including *The Faithful Hunter*; *Wind Eagle*; *Fox Song*; the Keepers of the Earth series; *The Boy Who Lived with the Bears*, a *Boston Globe–Horn Book* Honor Book; *Dog People*, winner of the Paterson Children's Writing Award; and *Many Nations: An Alphabet of Native America*, winner of an International Reading Association Teachers' Choice Award. The cofounder of *Greenfield Review Press*, he lives with his wife in upstate New York.

Amy Ehrlich, the editor of *When I Was Your Age, Volume Two*, says, "I so much enjoyed working on the first collection of ten stories that I wanted to do more. Both books were like surprise packages because I never knew what I was going to get. Each time a new story came in, I was amazed by its content and by just how good it was!"